Jill Roe has always written, but sometimes 'only in her head' rather than on paper. In 1993, she was the winner of a writing competition in the *Mail on Sunday* and this encouraged her to write seriously. Born in West Cornwall, she now lives with her husband in Avon and has five grandchildren. Her first novel, *Angels Flying Slowly*, was published last year and is also available from Sceptre.

SCEPTRE

A
New
Leaf

JILL ROE

SCEPTRE

First published in 1996 by Hodder and Stoughton
First published in paperback in 1996 by Hodder and Stoughton
A division of Hodder Headline PLC
A Sceptre Paperback

British Library Cataloguing in Publication Data

Roe, Jill
  New leaf
  I. Title
  823 [F]

  ISBN 0 340 65437 6

Typeset by Palimpsest Book Production Limited,
Polmont, Stirlingshire
Printed and bound in Great Britain by
Cox and Wyman Ltd, Reading, Berkshire

Hodder and Stoughton
A division of Hodder Headline PLC
338 Euston Road
London NW1 3BH

For Bryan and Mary Thirsk

∫

'We'll always tell each other everything, won't we Binnie? All our utter, utter secrets. Promise.' And Binnie, secretive in a way that Katha would never be, nodded agreement not even bothering to cross her fingers, having learned already that life is made up of secrets. Tiny secrets flickering like silverfish in the dark places of the mind and never to be shared with anyone, and big, joyful secrets, magnified and heightened by being allowed to escape and encompass everyone in the pleasure of their release. Unimportant, odd little secrets; dark ones, shameful even, and the secrets which formed a raft of truth and which she knew even then, were the foundation on which many lives were built and made bearable by concealment. Not by lies, which she knew to be wrong, but by the strength of secrecy which covered truth in a softer, sweeter coating like the chocolates which came in such numbers to her uncle's vicarage every Christmas.

1

November

Less than two hours before her husband's funeral Binnie Seaton was on the beach. To be a widow at forty might have been considered a misfortune but to Binnie it was as if a life sentence had been commuted and commuted, moreover, on account of her good behaviour.

It was a winter's day, the wind blowing briskly off the sea over small rough fields which blurred almost casually into cliffs at the very edge of Cornwall. Binnie had walked to the point where the beach turned round on itself, pebbly sand giving way to large rocks, the cliff rising in grey tiers towards a sky the blue of old delphiniums. She could smell wet seaweed and see gulls dropping like stones onto the water.

As Binnie walked she watched her bare feet making sudden dry circles in the sand where it stretched to the sea in ripples like corrugated iron, silver water lying in each furrow. She walked along the tide line, so intent on the curl and turn of each wave that she didn't see Katha climbing down the cliff path and it was only when a shadow fell in front of her that Binnie looked up.

'For God's sake Binnie, what are you doing? People are starting to arrive at the house and they're asking where you are. I've told them that you're resting – prostrate with grief.' Katha jumped back, out of the way of the splash and foam of a large wave which curled round Binnie's ankles. Binnie said nothing so Katha tried again. 'That bitch Pammie Brighton is sure to be there and I couldn't bear it if she thought she'd won and you *know* how good she looks in black. Anyway, think of Jory, he needs you there. Can't you at least pretend you're sorry about Richard?'

The water was so cold that Binnie's legs felt as if they were burning: her feet were numb and she didn't feel the grate and prick of sand on stone, pain would come later with the return of sensation. She turned reluctantly to walk up the beach, Katha's reminder of her son surprising her with guilt.

'I'd almost forgotten about Jory and I should be with him, you're absolutely right.' Binnie linked her arm through her friend's and they walked to where a pile of fallen rocks formed uneven steps to the cliff path. A collection of multicoloured debris was scattered amongst the seaweed left by the last high tide: pieces of frayed rope, empty bottles, an odd shoe, sodden and sad. Binnie bent down and pulled a plastic doll out of the tangle. It was speckled with tar and missing both arms but she was startled to find that the hard, round eyes still moved, and she tipped the doll backwards and forwards, watching their grotesque lift and fall.

'Looks just like Pammie,' she said and threw the doll with all her strength, following its arc high over the rocks until it fell face down in purple-shadowed seaweed. She looked at Katha.

'You know I'm sorry that Richard's dead, although it's mainly for Jory's sake. There were so many women, so many years, that I acquired a habit of indifference and I can't just shed it like a skin because it's not convenient.

I feel – oh, I don't know, not free exactly, but as if I've had my life given back to me: I wish you could understand Katha.'

Katha, who understood better than anyone how much Richard had hurt Binnie, handed her the boots she had left on the topmost step when she had walked down to the sea. Binnie leaned against the weathered wooden handrail to steady herself and forced her damp feet into resisting wellingtons and knew that already Richard belonged to the past. She followed Katha up the steep path prepared to carry out her duties as Richard's widow with her mind secretly acknowledging a guilty excitement about the future.

'I'll drive round the house and you can go up the back stairs to change.' Katha began to laugh. 'If you could see yourself Belinda Carter', Katha used Binnie's maiden name, 'your hair unkempt and tar all over your hands.' She spoke in the voice of their old headmistress but Binnie only smiled, her mood changing as swiftly as the weather at the sight of the several cars already parked at Jericho. She tried not to look at the space in front of the house left empty for the hearse and noticed with detachment that it had started to rain.

Katha's car pulled quietly into the yard and Sadie Clements, crossing the road with her shopping, noticed it with interest. She turned the corner of Trewavas Terrace and walked down the back lane to her own gate, putting one of her heavy bags down on the wet ground while she tried to disengage the two pieces of the catch. A push with her shoulder and the gate scraped open, a pebble caught underneath. As Sadie had passed her neighbour's house a spiral of blue smoke from behind the heavy cream nets had betrayed Cora Neville's watchful presence.

The early morning brightness had already dissipated, the weather settling back into its familiar pattern. It was a damp day in a week of dampness, the grey stone of the houses glistening in the rain, the roads wet enough for cars to send spray curving from their wheels: even the sea had disappeared in a soft grey haze which muffled the sound of waves breaking on the shingle.

There were no back gardens in Trewavas Terrace but each house had a yard with a whitewashed wall into which was set a wooden gate which opened into a back lane. The back lanes were the secret roadways of everyone who lived in the rows of terraces which stretched along behind the sea front and which twisted and curled into the hidden alleys where visitors strayed only by accident.

Cora Neville, who lived next door to Sadie Clements, had been watching for her return. Now she lit another cigarette and walked along the lane from her own yard gate to Sadie's house. She tapped on the back door and let herself into the kitchen.

'Shan't be five minutes Cora; make yourself a cup of tea if you want to, while I change. It's not worth taking the car is it? By the time we find somewhere to park we'll have to walk nearly as far as if we'd walked anyway. Oh Cora! I keep thinking of poor Binnie; do you think all those dreadful women will come?'

'I do hope so, it won't be half as much fun if they don't, and if you don't hurry up we shan't get a good seat.'

'Cora!' Sadie was genuinely shocked. Cora lit another cigarette, her eyes half shut as she watched her friend through the blue smoke. Sadie had finished putting away her shopping and went quickly upstairs to change, her flow of chatter silenced for once by Cora's flippancy.

I suppose it's because of Hannah, Sadie thought as she reached for her navy blue skirt and blazer; if you have to live with something like that I suppose it alters your outlook on everything. A picture of her own three handsome children came into her mind and she felt true sorrow for Cora, whose beautiful silky-haired Hannah would remain for ever a child.

She found a black silk scarf and took a large handkerchief from the pile in Charlo's drawer. When she went downstairs there were three stubs in the ashtray and the kitchen was full of the smell of cigarettes.

The rain had settled into an unremitting drizzle and Sadie wondered if they had been wise to walk to the church. She never managed to walk in the rain without splashing the back of her legs and she wished that she had Cora's disregard of others' opinions, for Cora wore soft, loose trousers and a black shawl, her long hair tied back by a velvet ribbon.

They passed the gates of Jericho, rhododendron bushes on either side of the drive dripping with dismal persistence. There were several cars parked near the house.

'Whose cars are those do you suppose Cora? They must belong to Richard's family because I don't think Binnie has any family left has she? Not since her aunt and uncle died anyway. I've never heard her talk of anyone, not even a cousin.'

Sadie was hurrying to keep up with Cora and her words came out a little breathlessly. 'I met her aunt and uncle once at a garden party at the Cathedral, he was Dean or something but they seemed very ordinary to me and yet Binnie's absolutely *loaded* according to Gwen Minto. She says the market garden and the house both belong to her.'

The church was on a hill overlooking the harbour and now and again as they splashed on through the rain they caught glimpses of the sea. The tide had turned and the surface of the water was the colour of a wood pigeon under the overcast sky. As they stood shaking raindrops from their umbrellas in the shelter of the porch, a surprisingly clean Range Rover drew up and a woman stepped out. She passed them without acknowledgement and Sadie's voice dropped almost to a whisper as she clutched Cora's arm.

'Do look Cora, it's that Pamela Brighton. What a nerve, marching in like that. You know she was with Richard when he died don't you? I hadn't realised she was so *plain*: poor old Binnie.'

High heeled black suede shoes, unmarked by any rain, moved up the blue carpet almost to the front of the church as Pammie Brighton, acknowledged trollop and erstwhile mistress of Richard Seaton, took her place among the mourners.

A fitted black jacket had been exchanged for her usual blue and heather tweed, but the long skirt, dark tights and navy hat were just as she wore them when judging at Horse Shows. The only concession she had made to the occasion was to have removed the twisted coloured band from the crown of her hat and to have forsaken her sensible navy shoes.

Pammie Brighton was small and light boned: her hair hanging shining and loose to her shoulders still with all its fiery brightness, as bright as the fox-coloured eyes which challenged so overtly: smooth creamy skin not yet coarsened by the high colour of broken veins, which would surely come in middle age. Women disliked her at once, men more reluctant to allow that such fragility could hide impenetrable ruthlessness.

For Richard's funeral she wore black kid gloves that covered the large, rough hands which were her only visible flaw and the price she paid for caring for her horses. It was generally accepted that she had the best seat in the county.

Sadie could see the Master sitting near the front of the church. He had been leading the field when Drummer, Richard's old bay hunter, had misjudged a hedge that he had jumped many times before and Richard had fallen hard, his neck broken by one of the granite stones that littered the fields around Rosmorran Farm. It had been Pammie who sat holding his hand while the soft rain enclosed them like a blanket and Pammie who stumbled beside the stretcher through the muddy ruts to the ambulance waiting in the lane. That Richard should die with Pammie at his side was the involuntary betrayal that Binnie found hard to forgive.

The church was already too full for comfort and Cora, squashed between Sadie and a pillar of green serpentine, longed desperately for a cigarette. Sadie was looking around the church; there were faces unfamiliar to her but many more that she recognised and Cora thought with amusement of the hours of entertainment the relaying of their singular histories would afford her friend.

Until you knew Sadie very well, her intelligence and acute observation remained obscured by the flow of seemingly inconsequential chatter but Cora had learned long ago to listen carefully to Sadie.

As Binnie and her son walked behind the coffin, Cora thought how tired Jory looked, his pallor emphasised by the dark red dye he had used to colour hair which she knew to be already turning grey. He reminded her of someone but it was so faint an impression, so slight, that it was gone almost before she acknowledged it.

Sadie leaned towards her and whispered, 'Good job Richard's being cremated; all this rain, just think what the cemetery would be like.'

Cora shifted in her uncomfortable seat and whispered back, 'And they can't very well sound *Gone to Ground* in the crematorium, can they?'

2

December

Binnie stood in the empty greenhouse, a memory of the smell of sunbaked leaves surrounding her like the essence of summer. 'All these years,' she thought, 'and I still can't eat tomatoes.'

There was a notebook on the bench and she picked it up. Richard's difficult writing detailed deliveries and telephone numbers and suddenly, for the first time since he had died, she felt anguish, immeasurable and unexpected.

She slid open the door and stepped into the night air. It was very quiet, thick old hedges cutting out noise from traffic along the main road. Binnie stood shivering, looking at the garden, at everything made unknown and extraordinary by the silver light of an almost full moon. Tomorrow she would go and see James, tell him that she was going to sell Jericho.

James Seaton was Richard's elder brother, so like him that Binnie always had to fight an impulse to love him as she would have loved Richard.

'But my dear, what will you do without Jericho?' James was concerned.

'Wear funny hats and arrange flowers. Do a spot of shoplifting. Do nothing. I don't know; I just know that I don't want to stay there any more.'

'What about Jory?' He hesitated, 'Surely Jericho should be his?'

'"His father's house" you mean? Dear James, you know very well that Jericho is mine, every daffodil and every damn tomato is mine. I suppose that even Richard's horses are mine as well really.' There was a silence.

'And Jory?'

Binnie looked steadily at James. In nearly twenty years it was the closest he had ever come to asking her about her son and she knew that he would never ask again.

'Of course,' she said, 'John Rory is mine too.' The words lay between them as nebulous as the mist that sometimes rose swiftly from the sea and crept over the land. The silence was easy and they sat together, detached but comfortable in their separate thoughts.

James stood up. 'I know that you've had a hard time, my dear, and I'm full of admiration for the way you stuck by Richard. I wish that things had been different but it's all over and he's gone now, poor fellow.' He looked down at her, taller than Richard, less handsome. 'I won't try and dissuade you from selling Jericho if that's what you think you should do and if you need any help, I'll do all I can.'

James turned towards the windows. They opened onto a small garden paved with cracked red tiles which were now green and slippery with moss. In summer the edges were softened by cushions of saxifrage and alchemilla and the dark hedge which surrounded the garden was overgrown by a small yellow rose, bright and fragrant. James had never known its name but had loved it since he was a child.

He didn't turn round, but Binnie heard him say, 'I've always been fond of Jory, you know. You will make sure he keeps in touch?'

When Binnie left James she felt melancholy, reluctant to leave the warm, beautiful house that had been Richard's childhood home and which now belonged to his brother. James had no son to succeed him and Binnie had always been aware of his unspoken deprivation. She almost wished that he hadn't mentioned Jory; he was their son, hers and Richard's, their only child whom they both loved deeply, but she knew that it wasn't right for James to think of leaving Owles Court to him.

She took the long way home, driving slowly up towards the croft land on the hill. The rain, which seemed to have persisted for weeks, had soaked the earth and lay in little, shining lakes on the fields. She parked the car beside a barn used to store hay and looked down the valley. The rain had stopped but a haze rose from the damp ground, wrapping winter-dark hedges in folds of grey. There was a line of bare, black trees on the horizon and as she watched, a cloud of rooks rose into the air turning and twisting as if they had practised their display. At the bottom of the hill was a farmhouse and Binnie could see cows in a muddy yard.

Lights came on in the house and she realised the day had slipped quietly into dusk while she sat there, watching the distant, small figures moving about their evening work. A blue pick-up had come into the yard; the cows had been driven in for milking; a dog had chased something unseen into the barn, and she had watched as if it was important to let nothing escape the camera of her mind. Binnie wished suddenly that she could walk down the hill, through the gorse bushes which even at this dark end of the year showed clusters of golden flowers among the thorns; across the muddy farmyard, to push open the door of the lighted house, wiping her feet on the old sack she was sure she would find just inside. She would warm her back against the Rayburn and sit down to pasties and junket and mugs of strong, sweet tea while the wet dogs crept round the fire and the dark and damp were part of a world shut out until morning.

She felt overwhelmed by her need to be with people, so unfamiliar a feeling that she hardly recognised it. She had been reluctant to allow anyone to see how often Richard left her on her own and concealment had developed in her a taste for solitude, but now she wanted more than anything to sit and observe other people living their lives, unseen but present like a ghost.

She was cold and started the car, waiting while the warm air cleared the windscreen before turning back the way she had come and driving home along the road by the sea. Strings of coloured lights left from the summer and which would be lit again at Christmas, swayed and rattled in a wind which was bringing more rain from the sea.

Tonight she would talk to Jory; they would decide together about selling Jericho and finding somewhere smaller where they could live. She felt sure he wouldn't mind: since he was seven years old Jory had wanted nothing except to go into the navy and the sooner he could leave behind the routine of sowing and picking and carting boxes to the Growers' Co-op the happier he would be.

As Binnie stopped outside Jericho, Ralph Minto came out from the small greenhouse and swung the gate open for her, waving acknowledgement as he turned up the road towards Zion House.

Zion House was larger than the other houses in the terrace, not by merit of being detached but because it was on a corner and where the road curved gently facing the gardens of Jericho, Ralph Minto and his mother Gwen had built three rooms on the long side and now opened their home to paying guests.

Jericho's gardens ran the length of the road, the house itself standing back, stranded like some sea creature when the tide of development had encroached on its land a hundred years before. Where the rose garden had once drenched the evening air with sweetness there were now rows of salad vegetables. In the spring there were narcissi and daffodils and throughout the summer the greenhouses were full of tomatoes, their coarse stalks staining an ineradicable yellow the hands of anyone working with them.

This was often Ralph Minto. He had liked Richard Seaton and found no incongruity in working for a friend. There was always something he could do and although Richard was dead, Ralph would continue to work for Binnie, whom he loved almost as much, and with as little physical passion, as he loved his mother.

Ralph washed his hands and sat down at the kitchen table, waiting for his mother to tell him what their new boarder had wanted to talk to her about just before he had slipped out the back way to go to Jericho. Gwen put a cup of tea in front of him.

'That woman, Ralph, do you know what it was this time? "Oh, Mrs Minto",' Gwen was a good mimic and Dixie Davey's carefully modulated voice spoke in the kitchen, '"as you know, I don't really eat breakfast, except for toast and cornflakes, and as you advertise a full English breakfast, I wondered if you might care to make a small reduction in my weekly terms".'

'What did you say?' Ralph was amused.

'I told her that she was already getting a reduction as it's out of season and that I had a business to run and if she found our terms too much for her I could always recommend Mrs Jago down by the station. I think she's got something up her sleeve, Ralph; I shall watch out for her.'

When Dixie Davey had first appeared on the doorstep of Zion House, Ralph had felt a premonition of trouble. He was a placid and pragmatic man, not usually given to such feelings but perhaps it was the face of Sid Hoskin as he struggled to unload two old and heavy leather suitcases from his taxi that gave rise to Ralph's unease. Dixie's voice had rung out in the quiet afternoon as she tried to find a ten pence piece in her purse.

'Thank you so much, I couldn't possibly have managed them on my own.' She handed Sid the exact fare. 'I'm frightfully sorry but I don't seem to have any spare change. I'll be sure to remember next time.'

She had picked up several Harrods carrier bags, encompassing Ralph in her accomplished, confident smile as she walked past him into the house.

While Gwen put sprouts and mashed potatoes into cracked and beautiful dishes, Ralph read the letter she had left on the table for him.

'Enys Williams,' he said, 'the name sounds familiar; and he says that he wants to stay here while he looks for a house to buy. Hmm.'

'His grandparents used to live down the road at Tiverton Villa. They'd sold it by the time we came here but you've probably heard the name. I think he stayed with them during the war but his mother remarried when his father was killed and they moved up country somewhere.'

She put a steak and kidney pie on the table, golden pastry fluted round the edge, steam escaping through the open mouth of a china blackbird. Half of its beak was missing.

'We don't often have two guests out of season. Would you mind the extra work?'

'If you give me a hand to turn out a room, I'll manage all right.' Gwen smiled at her son and passed him the gravy.

At sixty-six Gwen Minto was a pretty woman. Her face was round and sweet, the soft skin beginning to shrink like a slowly drying apple, wrinkles criss-crossing her cheeks when she smiled. Little lines ran upwards from her eyes and across her eyelids over gentle blue eyes which often sparkled with merriment. There wasn't, as her friend Pearl Angove said, an unkind bone in Gwen Minto's body.

Ralph and Gwen lived together in placid understanding. If Ralph sometimes sought less tranquil company, Gwen chose to disregard it: if Gwen sometimes called him by his father's name, Ralph overlooked the slip. His father had died when he was younger than Ralph was now and the resemblance between them was so marked that Gwen looked forward to seeing in Ralph the husband who had never aged.

'This Enys Williams,' Ralph looked at the letter, thick white paper, a few lines in spiky black writing, 'was he down here this past summer, do you remember?'

'Yes, I believe he must have been because Pearl told me that she saw him standing on the pavement looking at his grandparents' house oh, three or four months ago. She said that she recognised him at once – all the Williams had that funny hair – and she said he looked just like he used to when he was a little boy and wanted to play outside with the other children but his grandparents wouldn't let him out of the garden.

'Pearl asked him in for a cup of tea but she didn't get much out of him except that he had recently left the army and was thinking of moving back to Cornwall. I thought I'd already told you all about it.'

Gwen was clearing the table as she spoke and now put a dish of whisked jelly in front of Ralph. The jelly was very green and smelled, Ralph thought, like Jeyes Fluid.

Gwen was going to the Womens' Bright Hour which Pearl organised on Wednesday evenings in the meeting room which was part of the chapel on the corner where her husband was the minister. Everyone knew that it was really Pearl who ran the parish and tonight she had arranged a talk called 'How to Make Your Own Christmas Crackers', with a prize for the most original joke.

Gwen always left the washing up for Ralph on Wednesday evenings and as she went to get ready she stopped half way up the stairs, puzzled by a faint smell of curry. She wasn't at all interested in learning how to make Christmas crackers but she wanted to ask Pearl about Enys Williams. It was the thought of the small wistful boy watching other children playing that had touched her soft heart and if he was going to stay in her house she wanted to know more about him. Pearl would know, Pearl knew everything.

Pearl Angove had a very direct way of looking at anyone, her head with its harshly dyed hair tilted slightly backwards and her small mouth pursed. It was as if she already knew the truth and was waiting to reach out, to tease and then catch it, like a cat with a bird. Most people were afraid of her and she became used to seeing her husband's parishioners suddenly engrossed in a window display as she approached, or hearing stumbling excuses made for unavailability.

Gwen alone remained unaffected by her sharp tongue and condemnation of others' behaviour for Gwen was the only person who had seen bruises as green and mauve as a ripe fig on the soft white part of Pearl's arms before she had time to pull down her sleeves and button the cuffs around her wrists. Gwen had looked at Pearl standing in front of the old-fashioned wooden draining board she had been scrubbing, her sleeves rolled up and an apron made from a jumble sale dress stretched over her oddly keel-shaped chest, and understood at once why she had never liked the Reverend Wilfred Angove. They never spoke of this shared knowledge but Pearl's appraisals became more moderate when she was with Gwen and Gwen, in time, learned to appreciate her friend's fortitude and loyalty.

While Ralph did the washing up he thought about Binnie, letting his mind wander through the greenhouses, full of pots of early, tender flowers, and he remembered the tiresome job of planting the corms and bulbs with Richard in the autumn. He would miss Richard, miss his reminiscent laugh as he recalled for Ralph some escapade with one of the Dickie Birds. Sometimes, listening to Richard, Ralph was glad that he had never suffered from the discomfort of love although he realised that his life was missing a dimension, an intensity of feeling that he found hard to imagine.

Binnie had looked so odd and distant when he had opened the gate for her earlier that evening that he had changed his mind about speaking to her then, but Ralph could see what needed to be done if the flowers were to be ready to send up to London to get the best prices at Christmas and he decided to walk over to Jericho.

He knocked on the back door and it was opened at once. The remains of a meal were on the kitchen table; strips of some kind of green pasta had been pushed to the edge of one of the plates, scrambled together with peppers and tomatoes in a congealed lump.

'Coffee, Ralph?' Jory waved a mug in his direction. 'I'm glad you've come. I want to go out and I think Mum needs company. She's thinking of selling Jericho, did you know? I don't mind as I'm off to Dartmouth anyway, but I do worry about what Mum will do on her own.' He filled three mugs and Ralph, perfectly at home in Binnie's house, went to the cupboard for sugar.

'Aunt Katha was coming over but she's hurt her back, turning a sheep or something. Sounds disgusting.' Jory grinned and Ralph heard him thumping up the stairs, released from responsibility for the evening.

Binnie must have heard him coming in. As he walked along the passage to where a strip of pale light showed under the door of Richard's study she called out, 'Door's open, Ralph.' She was sitting at the roll-topped desk, account books and papers spread around her in controlled confusion and Ralph settled himself on the slippery horsehair sofa that Richard had insisted on keeping in the study. It was Katha who had named it the 'Casting Couch' and Binnie had been determined to get rid of it as soon as she could. 'Jory told you that I'm going to sell Jericho?'

'He said you're thinking of it – are you?'

Binnie nodded and drank some of the coffee Ralph had brought with him. Jory made good coffee, better than the odd meal he had prepared for their supper. Pasta and vegetables, too oily and overcooked. She had been grateful to him but not hungry, feeling self-pity welling up inside her, knowing Jory wanted to meet Jassy Clements and walk with her along the windswept promenade to the warmth and shelter of The Ship.

Binnie had closed the wooden shutters over the windows and switched on only the lamp with the curling brass neck like a swan's that stood on the desk next to an inkstand made from the hoof of Richard's first pony. Binnie would throw that away with the sofa, it made her shudder each time she looked at it. In the dim light the small room was cosy; Ralph was sitting outside the circle of illumination and she couldn't see his face clearly, only the heavy brown brogues he always wore.

'Everyone says I should wait before making any big decisions like selling the market garden but I knew years ago that I didn't enjoy it any more. It was just that it gave Richard the illusion of working and providing for us.' She moved some papers around on the desk and looked at Ralph with a small smile. 'Perhaps I should have married a foreign playboy who would've been happy to take my money without having to feel he was earning it, but the puritan conscience doesn't work like that, does it?'

Ralph shifted on the uncomfortable sofa. 'Did Richard have a puritan conscience?'

'Of course not. I think he had,' Binnie sought for a word

that kept eluding her, 'a *selective* conscience, wouldn't you say? But I got so tired, Ralph, having to load the pick-up and go to the Co-op with all those boxes of tomatoes when Richard promised to be back to do it, and never was. I was tired of the women on the phone, pretending to be leaving an order when *I* answered; tired of guests whom Richard had invited, sitting around waiting for him to appear while dinner spoiled.'

Ralph remembered some of those dinners, beef hardening in the oven, soufflés deflated, as Binnie struggled to keep afloat conversations that recovered only when Richard arrived, penitent and charming, winning over nearly everyone with practised ease. In spite of everything he knew about him, Ralph had liked Richard, amused by his wickedness; envious, perhaps, of the facility with which he lied. He wondered if Binnie had really loved him and had just become inured to the incursions into her happiness.

A habit of decency had always kept Ralph from offering physical comfort to Binnie and he hid his tenderness and pity for her behind a mask of friendship, never breached on either side. He knew that if he had ever loved any woman it was Binnie, but love was something that Ralph knew only in the abstract.

His mother often said she wished that he would get married and out from under her feet, and the girls Ralph had brought home when he was a younger man had been warmly welcomed by Gwen but none had managed to prise Ralph from his mother, and one by one they had married other men, bad tempered or unfaithful, and thought yearningly of life as it would have been with quiet, dependable Ralph.

Binnie had stopped talking and Ralph waited to see if she had more to say. The room still smelled of Richard, a mixture of saddle soap and leather and the lingering undertone of Bay Rum that he sometimes used on his hair.

Paintings and photographs of horses and hounds hung all around the dark green walls, now lost in the darkness but underlining thirty years of Richard's life when daylight filled the room.

'Shall I just carry on as usual then, Binnie? Do you want to sell the early flowers or are you not going to bother?'

'Oh.' Binnie looked as if she had forgotten that Ralph was there, 'Yes. Yes please, but once the earlies are finished we'd better talk about it again.'

It was a cold, clear night and as Ralph crossed the road he could see Orion's Belt high in the sky. As he watched, the lights went out in the chapel meeting room and once in the warmth of the kitchen he put a pan of milk ready to heat for his mother's Horlicks and poured himself a whisky. He hated change but he was going to have to get used to it. Tomorrow he would start disbudding the flowers and put thoughts of Jericho with a new owner out of his mind.

He heard Dixie Davey's key in the front door and turned off the kitchen light; the last thing he wanted tonight was the relentless cheeriness of their new boarder.

Dixie let herself into Zion House as quietly as she could. She had made a show of reluctance, not altogether feigned, when Gwen Minto had pressed an invitation on her to go as Gwen's guest to the Bright Hour: it had been a tedious evening, but not entirely a waste of time. Always the first to volunteer, she had started washing up almost before the Reverend Wilfred had finished blessing the evening. She had been humming very quietly to herself, deliberately preoccupied, as conversation flowed around her.

Nothing of importance was ever discussed in the meeting room; the kitchen, smelling of old tea and old women, was where everything that really mattered was reviewed, disputed and decided. Feuds, stifled in public, broke out in all their acrimony once the door had been closed between the meeting room, redolent of a hundred jumble sales, and the small damp kitchen.

Sometimes the air seemed full of spite, insinuations dripped around the listeners like the condensation which trickled down the window panes. It was here where whispered rumour and truth mingled inextricably, that Dixie Davey was at home. By being very still, she heard the bitterness of truth, of discontent, that lay hidden under spurious good humour. She listened and remembered and spoke with cheerful insincerity.

Tonight the talk had been of Enys Williams. The older women who attended the Bright Hour remembered his grandparents and the small boy who had stayed with them during the war.

'Always thought herself a cut above everybody else that Olive Williams and dear knows why, she wasn't no better than a ladies' maid for all she called herself a "companion".'

Ruby Daniels, heavy and moustached and with eyes like gooseberries, scoured a plate with a soggy tea towel and laughed, a small unpleasant sound. 'An' that son of hers, gave *him* ideas too – fancy calling her boy Enys, what's wrong with Derek or Mervyn like anyone else? If it hadn't been for that funny hair I'd have wondered if he was a Williams at all.'

There was a titter of laughter from Ruby's friends and Dixie, fishing for the last teaspoon in the murky water, smiled secretly to herself.

She had walked home on her own, not waiting for Gwen, and had seen the light go off in the kitchen as her key scraped in the lock: Ralph must be in but she had work to do and she moved quickly up the stairs, drawing the curtains before putting on the light.

From one of her two leather suitcases she took a large, out-of-date diary which she had bought for twenty pence in an Oxfam shop somewhere along the south coast. The first half of the diary detailed the achievements of a century of performance by a company selling patent medicines and served Dixie very well as a diversion from its true purpose.

She opened the dark padded cover, found a clean page and printed ENYS WILLIAMS. She underlined it in red and settled down to write.

Pearl Angove was the last to leave the meeting room and lingered needlessly, gathering up tea towels and checking the urn she knew to be empty. She hoped to give her husband enough time to be home before her so she could slip quietly in the back door without disturbing him. Ruby Daniels though, always delayed the Reverend Wilfred after the Bright Hour with a breathy disclosure too confidential to be spoken until they were alone and as Pearl locked the meeting room door and walked along the dark, mossy pathway to the road she saw her husband and the bulk that was Ruby Daniels standing and talking, Wilfred Angove giving Ruby his full attention. He nodded several times then thanked her for her vigilance, promising to consider what she had told him. He touched her on the shoulder and turned away with a wave and an almost teasing expression as he followed his wife into the house.

As soon as he had closed the door behind Pearl, Wilfred Angove turned towards her, the caring, compassionate smile gone, replaced by an expression of contempt, his eyes magnified to a plastic hardness by the lenses of his spectacles. Pearl tried to slide by him but he caught her by the arm and swung her against the newel post at the bottom of the stairs. 'You needn't think your job's finished for the evening,' he said, menace in his voice, 'get upstairs and wait for me; it's all you're good for, after all.'

As Pearl walked upstairs, determined not to let Wilfred

see that her side was aching where she had crashed against the wood, she envied Gwen Minto going home to warm Horlicks and a soft, comfortable bed. Even Ruby Daniels, malicious, unloveable Ruby Daniels, wrung a grudging envy from Pearl Angove as she unzipped her shabby brown crimplene skirt and crawled between the sheets, careful with her bruised ribs. Ruby had her fat and lazy pug to take for a walk before she went to bed, an interdependence of affection that Pearl would have exchanged for her own situation as she heard Wilfred's footsteps on the thinly carpeted stairs.

3

March

'Several letters for you this morning, Mrs Davey.' Gwen put a rack of toast on the yellow-checked tablecloth and three letters beside Dixie's plate. The toast rack was the only surviving part of a Clarice Cliff breakfast set that Gwen had been given as a wedding present and was only slightly chipped.

Gwen was curious about Dixie's post. Most of her letters were re-addressed to Zion House and occasionally, as this morning, one arrived sent directly but written by the same hand. It was the number of letters Dixie received that engaged Gwen's curiosity.

'This will be from my mother,' Dixie said, 'I thought she would enjoy a little holiday with me while I'm down here. I must speak to you about it, Mrs Minto, and come to some arrangement about terms – I expect there would be a reduction for two people?'

'I'm afraid not, Mrs Davey but I could offer to move you into the two rooms at the top of the house. Is your mother, well – sprightly?'

Dixie snapped a piece of toast into two symmetrical halves.

'Oh yes Mrs Minto, I think you could call her "sprightly". Very "sprightly" indeed. I'll let you know.'

Dismissed, Gwen went back to the kitchen and started to fry eggs and bacon for Ralph's breakfast. Ralph enjoyed breakfast and now he came into the kitchen as pink and clean as a child after his shower. He poured two cups of strong tea while Gwen lifted eggs like frilled lace from the pan.

She opened the back door and put the bacon rinds on top of the wall for the birds. There had been rain in the night but now the air was fresh, a few clouds in a high blue sky and the smell of the sea blown in on the wind. Big herring gulls screeched as they floated and scavenged over the backyards, coming to rest on roofs and chimney pots.

'You'll have all those shite hawks down in the yard if you put scraps out, Mother.'

'Ralph!' Gwen rather liked the expression but gentle reprimand was a habit between them. She was looking across the road to the thick hedges sheltering the market garden and she wondered what Binnie was doing. Ralph had told her that Jericho was to be sold but she hadn't pressed him for details, seeing more in his face than his words would say.

Her attention was held by a man walking along the footpath in the shelter of the hedge. She knew who it was: only one person had that odd, lopsided way of moving and Gwen stepped back quickly into the kitchen and closed the door.

'Did you know Doddy Rowe was home again?' she asked Ralph, who was removing specks of butter from the jar of marmalade in front of him.

'I suppose he must be, he only got six months this time didn't he? I wish you'd use a spoon for the marmalade Mother, I hate bits of butter stuck in it.' He wiped his knife on the edge of his plate. 'Did he look as if he was going to Binnie's? I'd better go in case there's any trouble.'

Gwen opened the back door to look out again and gasped. Doddy Rowe was standing on the step, his hand raised.

'Mornin' missus, Ralph in is 'e?' He looked round her. 'How'r'e doin' then boy? Come for me old job back.'

'Grand, thanks Doddy,' Ralph wiped his mouth, 'but I'm afraid there's no job for you. Perhaps you didn't know that Richard Seaton's dead?'

''ess, 'ess, I 'eard that. I was some sorry, a grand chap, a grand chap.' He had stepped into the kitchen and looked as if he was thinking of pulling out a chair and sitting down at the table, but Gwen moved quickly and blocked his way.

Doddy Rowe was a shambling, middle aged teddy boy. His black hair was still sufficiently thick to allow him to comb it off his face in a greasy pompadour, away from eyes that always reminded Ralph of an orang-utan he had seen at London Zoo on a school trip years ago. Doddy wore tight black jeans and thick soled shoes. His curious sideways walk was the result of an accident one New Year's Eve when he had fallen over the harbour wall and had lain on the deck of a trawler until morning: his leg, broken in the fall, caused him increasing pain as he grew older.

Although he had spent the summer months out of the reach of sunshine, he was permanently tanned. His face with it's clown's eyes, was triangular, the forehead wide and bony, and he was always dirty; nails black-edged, hands ingrained with earth and fish guts and nicotine.

PC Darryl Lander, whose father had been at school with the Rowe brothers, was thankful to whatever providence looked after young policemen that it was Doddy and not his brother Jos who was loading what he described as 'scrap metal' into the back of a rusty Ford pick-up on the wet June evening when Darryl, sheltering from the horizontal summer rain, had slipped into a doorway behind the ships' chandlers for a smoke.

Doddy was a peaceful man so when he was caught in possession of an outboard motor or two, a few months' confinement had seemed to him merely unfortunate, although, given the choice, he preferred to spend the winter months in prison.

He had been sorry to hear about Richard Seaton. Richard was someone who had understood a man like Doddy Rowe and had given him work whenever he needed it. Ralph was a different matter altogether, not that it mattered now, of course.

'I'm so thirsty as a fish, missus.' Gwen fetched a thick white mug that she kept in the back scullery, for Doddy Rowe was no stranger to her kitchen. He was looking at the leathery toast left over from breakfast and Gwen spread butter on a slice and passed it to him, trying not to look at his filthy hands on her tablecloth.

'Tha's a proper job,' he said, his mouth full of toast, 'you'm a lucky bugger, Ralph, to have someone looking after you.' He sucked tea through his teeth and Gwen refilled his mug, but when he got out a tobacco tin and cigarette papers Ralph, seeing the look on his mother's face, stood up.

'Come on Doddy, I'll walk with you to the corner.' They went out together, Gwen watching from the doorway.

'How's that pretty little maid of yourn then Ralph? Always thought you 'ad your eye on she.' He laughed again, wheezing and coughing as they crossed the road.

'Listen to me Doddy,' Ralph put out his hand to grasp the other man's arm, changing his mind as he looked at the stained sleeve, 'don't push your luck. My mother may be a good Christian but I'm not. I can be very nasty if I feel like it and I'm beginning to feel like it now. You leave Binnie alone. Do you hear me?'

'Oh 'ess, 'ess, I 'ears you but there's a lot Doddy 'ears, lots

I sees too.' He looked sideways at Ralph, his eyes watchful under the quiff of black hair.

They had reached the gates of Jericho and Ralph took a handful of change out of his pocket, found three pound coins and handed them to Doddy. Doddy clamped his dirty fingers around them and limped down the escallonia-edged footpath in the direction of the main road.

Binnie had woken early from a dream of primroses in deep woods, where sunlight dappled the ground and birds crooned softly. She lay for a long time in the cocoon of warmth and softness that she no longer had to share.

It had been her habit since she was a child in her uncle's vicarage, to open the curtains before she got into bed at night and now, as she lay watching the sunlight of her dream turn into the reality of morning, she felt happiness, greater than she had experienced for a long time, spread through her like the pale light that drifted through the window. Detachment had become so familiar to her that she was surprised to find herself looking forward with gladness to a day of no particular significance. Ralph would come in for coffee, she would telephone the estate agent and then she would go into the attics and start to sort through the disregarded remnants of other peoples' lives.

Both she and Richard had come to Jericho with possessions that neither wanted and though the house had swallowed up furniture that they found unappealing, there were boxes that Binnie had never opened and which she had brought from the vicarage when her uncle had died and her aunt, whom she had loved so dearly, had slid gently into a world where Binnie could no longer reach her. If she were to move into a smaller house then she would need to compress the impedimenta of her life. In her present mood, even that thought pleased her.

Binnie sat on the wide window seat, wrapped in the

viyella dressing gown that she had worn for twenty years and looked across the lawn and yew hedge, seeing in her mind's eye the old garden, now ploughed and transformed, where flowers stood in the early Cornish spring in unnatural straight lines, to be picked in the bud and packed and sent to London: where lettuce and radish and spring onions grew and where three glasshouses protected tomatoes, endless tomatoes, to be taken to the Growers' Co-op and sent by rail to markets all over the country.

When Binnie had bought Jericho just after she and Richard were married, an overgrown and desolate garden lay all around the house, a new footpath joining the main road into town bisecting what had been the rose garden. The walls of the old kitchen garden were still there sheltering tender fruit in their warmth, but the paths had been demolished, the rank straggle of weeds falling to a flame-thrower before a cultivator had reduced the whole to a flat, umber plain.

Binnie would have preferred to live in the country but deferred, as always, to Richard when he said that a market garden was just what they wanted and Jericho was just the place to start one. If any resentment threatened to surface in her mind, she reminded herself of how grateful she was to Richard, although she wondered sometimes if their complicity ever caused him to question the way they lived. In time it ceased to matter very much: Richard's presence, his infidelities, even his increasingly frequent absences, causing her no more than irritation. She had begun a process of withdrawal.

Binnie had never ceased to yearn for the vanished garden and looked after the borders that she had made around the lawn with care and artistry. She had insisted that the hedge remained between the house and the market garden even though the sheltering band of fir trees had gone.

'Nothing will grow in their shade, Binnie,' Richard had

said and she had agreed reluctantly, watching the cream-coloured sawdust blowing around in the wind as the saw whined and bit through the old, soft trunks. Under the hedge she had preserved the illusion of a wild garden where celandines carpeted the grass with bold, bright flowers in the earliest spring days, where wood anemones and bluebells grew in the shade and traveller's joy twined along the hedge in autumn, silver awns clinging until they were blown away by a sudden vicious wind that sprang from the sea.

At first Richard had worked enthusiastically to establish the market garden, but he grew bored with routine and over the years Binnie had found herself taking on the day-to-day running of the business. She wouldn't allow herself to acknowledge the thought that she didn't need to do it, her years in the vicarage had taught her that it was important for Richard to be seen to be successful. She had watched her aunt lead a life of small, covert economies and self-denial, happy to live in the shadow of her husband, whose handsome face and comfortable clichés from the pulpit, ensured that the Reverend Basil Carter's congregation was at least intermittently faithful.

No one had ever explained to Binnie why she had been sent to live with Aunt Vee and Uncle Basil. She had heard her father speak of his elder brother but she had never met him before she arrived at the vicarage, bewildered and afraid and grieving for her parents. She wondered why her mother's sister hadn't found room for her in the house full of noisy cousins whom she knew, and it wasn't until she held Jory in her arms that she thought she understood why Aunt Vee had begged to be allowed to look after the little girl. Uncle Basil looked so like her father that she had made the mistake of behaving as she had always behaved, but Basil Carter was a shyer and more principled man than his brother and, although Binnie eventually came to appreciate the kindness and integrity cloaked by his reserve, she never found with him the spontaneity she enjoyed with her aunt.

She had travelled on her own from Paddington and waited anxiously in the long, glass-domed station but no one had come to meet her and she had decided that she must have misunderstood her aunt's letter. She walked out to the forecourt, found a taxi and asked shyly to be taken to St Euny's Vicarage. Aunt Vee had opened the heavy black door of the house which was to be her new home and held out her arms to the child standing forlornly on the gravel path.

'I thought your uncle was going to meet you, but I suppose he was waylaid again. That's the trouble with being a clergyman, either everyone wants to speak to you or no one does. You must have wondered why there was no one at the station but you were very sensible to take a taxi. Anyhow, you're here now and I'm *so glad* to have you. Come in and I'll show you your room.'

She picked up the little suitcase and together they walked up the wide staircase covered in a carpet so threadbare that patches of canvas showed through the red pattern.

'I've put you in a room where you can see the sea. It's rather a gloomy old house, I'm afraid, *much* too big for us and rather cold when the wind blows, but we do have nice views.'

Binnie looked around the room her aunt had prepared for her. The walls were the colour of rich milk and Vee had found beautiful curtains in a box of jumble and had taken them without a pang. They were made of stiff watermarked silk with a design of pink roses and blue bows, faded almost to white in places. She had hung the sun bleached strip next to the wall and dyed an old cotton counterpane as close to the colour of the roses as she could. There was a fireplace with a rusty iron firebasket, surrounded by tiles of startling emerald green, and a worn beige carpet, the worst patch covered by a rug. Vee had moved a chair and a desk out of one of the unused rooms and polished it's tapered legs and little fretwork panels until it shone.

She looked anxiously at the child. 'Is it all right for you Binnie? I do so want you to be happy here.'

Binnie had looked around the oddly furnished room and smiled and said, 'It's lovely Aunt Vee, thank you,' and when her aunt had gone down to put on the kettle for tea, she had sat on the bed and looked around her, thinking of the room in her parents' house, where a thick blue carpet had covered the floor and where there had been toys and bookshelves and a cupboard full of clothes. She had walked back along the passage to the stairs with their shabby carpet and found her aunt in the biggest, dimmest kitchen she had ever seen and they had sat together and eaten fairy cakes and sipped weak tea and she had begun to feel safe again.

For a long time Binnie had found it painful to think about her aunt's goodness and sweetness clouded by confusion as she drifted into a world where there was no longer any direction, no time nor recognition. Binnie had been pregnant when Aunt Vee died and she still felt a sense of loss that she had never been able to share Jory with her or for her to hold him in her arms and feel his downy, egg-shaped head against her cheek. Her own mother had become a shadow in her mind, her face in the fading photographs that Binnie had always young and smiling.

It wasn't until her uncle died that Binnie had discovered that she was rich. She had lived so long as a vicarage child, sharing the simple food, wearing home-made clothes and learning not to ask for anything not strictly necessary, while all the time the money that her parents had left her gathered interest from investments that her uncle had made.

'Your uncle had the same good brain as your father, you know, but I think he felt that your grandfather had made his money, well, *dubiously*, and he didn't feel comfortable about it but he *did* think it would be wrong not to look after the money that belonged to you and, just between us, I believe it gave him quite a lot of satisfaction, seeing your money grow. Good stewardship, he called it.'

'But, Aunt Vee, why didn't you use any of it? I know how much I must have cost you over the years and yet there was all that money there and you didn't touch it.'

'Well, that's not quite right Binnie. We did use some of it to pay for your school fees, but that was all. Your uncle didn't think your education should suffer just because we didn't have much money ourselves and I was *happy* to treat you just as if you had been our own child. We certainly couldn't have loved you any more if you had been.'

Binnie had never known what to do with her money. Until she met Richard, and then it had all seemed so simple.

When Binnie had dressed and gone downstairs, she found Jory's breakfast dishes were stacked neatly on the draining board, the saucepan in which he had made his porridge, filled with soapy water beside them. Binnie couldn't imagine any other boy of his age eating porridge every morning and certainly none of them leaving the kitchen so clean and tidy. It worried her a little.

She had heard Jory coming in last night as she lay watching the moon disappearing behind ragged clouds, emerging again with a pale halo around it. Rain on the way, she thought as she heard Jory moving quietly up the stairs. Her light was off so he didn't tap on her door and come and sit with her, as he often did when he had been out for the evening. She thought about Jassy Clements and Jory's infatuation with her, and all her instincts told her that Jory would be hurt.

She wondered if his friends found him dull; she was well aware that her friends found her so. Perhaps it was her dullness, her tractability, that had driven Richard away; the secrecy she had learned early as a way to protect herself from hurt, that made him look elsewhere for vivacity in his lovers.

When she listened to Sadie or Katha discussing their children, it became apparent to Binnie that Jory was unusual in never having given either her or Richard any cause for concern. When he was seven he had said that he was going to be a sailor and never have to grow another thing, ever. However, without much persuasion he had helped in the market garden, slipping away when he could to hang around the harbour and the Yacht Club, crewing for anyone who would take him out. He worked hard at school and passed his exams well enough; he sang with a local choir; he was polite and responsible and, Binnie had to admit it, rather dull.

She could understand why he was so attracted to Jassy. She was the prettiest and liveliest of all the girls that Jory knew. At eighteen, her small face still looked childish and her round, polished cheeks reminded Binnie of a pink and gold nectarine. Even Sadie, who fought exasperated battles with her, secretly knew that Jassy was enchanting. Her hair was mid-brown, bleached into golden highlights by the sun and she had small, very white, very even teeth. Sadie was firm with all her children but the golden little Jassy slipped through the bounds of discipline as easily as small fish through a net, smiling and laughing and with her brown eyes sparkling. Like Binnie, Sadie was afraid that Jassy would break Jory's heart.

4

April

'Anyone there? Coo-ee!' The voice was old and thin but carried into the kitchen where Gwen was making seedy cake for tea. Before she could untie the strings of her pinafore, there was another call.

'SHOP!' This was accompanied by the counterpoint of a small bell that stood on a serving table outside the dining room. Gwen slowed down as she walked along the passage from the kitchen to watch a very old woman standing in the hall who was looking through the pages of the Guests' registration book.

She was not only very old, but very small and very thin, dressed in a crimplene suit of what Gwen thought of as Barclays-Bank blue. Sheer grey stockings wrinkled down legs as thin as a child's towards white shoes with heels so high that her ankles leaned outwards as she walked. It was difficult to distinguish her hair from her hat, both being the colour and texture of candyfloss: large sunglasses hid her eyes.

The old woman held out a tiny wrinkled hand on which glittered several rings, which Gwen thought to be real. 'I'm

Mrs Lily Beagerie. I've come to stay with my daughter, Mrs Doreen Davey.'

'Oh, Mrs Beagerie I'm sorry but I don't think that Mrs Davey is back yet. You do mean Mrs *Dixie* Davey, don't you?'

Lily Beagerie gave a little snuffle. '*Dixie* is it now; well of course I mean *Dixie*, if that's what she's calling herself this time.' Almost without a pause she went on, 'I could do with a cuppa, stuff on the train was like gnat's pee.'

'Would you like to come into the guests' lounge to wait for your daughter, Mrs Beagerie and I'll bring you some tea, I was just going to make some.'

Gwen leaned against the kitchen table, seeing in her mind's eye the elegant, patronising figure of Dixie Davey with her leather handbags and silk scarves; hearing her confident, commanding voice disputing some item on her weekly account.

Ralph, coming in from the back yard, found his mother with tears of laughter in her eyes.

'You take the tea in Ralph and then you can see her. Oh my dear soul!' She started to laugh again.

Before Ralph had time to ask his mother what she meant there was a knock on the kitchen door and it was pushed open.

'It's only me. I thought I'd rather sit with you until Doreen gets back. Don't mind, do you? Got lonely on my own and we can get to know each other a bit. This your boy is it? I've heard all about *him*.' The glasses turned towards Ralph. 'Nice looking though.'

For once, her perfunctory judgement was right, Ralph *was* nice looking; from his disorderly sandy hair to his big brogue-shod feet, Ralph epitomised niceness. Although he was tall and broad, his clothes always looked as if they had been bought for an even bigger man. It wasn't that they didn't fit but he seemed to move about inside them, as if somehow he shrank away from their embrace, superfluous material left unused by his body.

He was fastidiously clean and always smelled of Imperial Leather soap, with which he scrubbed his big hands many times a day in an effort to rid them of stains from plants and soil.

Gwen did mind the intrusion into her kitchen, she minded quite a lot. No guest ever came uninvited into the part of the house where she and Ralph lived. She sighed, thinking how difficult it was sometimes to love one's neighbour. She supposed that even Doddy Rowe was a neighbour in that sense and now she had this bizarre old woman to look after as well.

'Do you know where Doreen's gone?'

'Mrs Davey? No, I'm afraid not. She doesn't usually say where she's going but depending on whether or not she's having her evening meal here, she gets back sometime in the afternoon.' She remembered again the whiff of curry on the stairs and the occasional lingering smell of fish and chips and made up her mind once more that she must speak to Dixie Davey about it.

Gwen found the big black sunglasses unnerving, as if she were talking to a doll, but Lily Beagerie seemed unaware of her exclusion. 'I expect she's been trying to get something knocked off her bill, hasn't she? Never known anyone like Doreen for getting something on the cheap. I shouldn't think she's paid full price for anything for years. Takes everything back and complains about it all – always gets her own way in the end.' Lily started to laugh but it turned into a cough, deep and wracking. She seemed exhausted by it and leaned back in her chair. When she had caught her breath she went on, 'She's always been good to me though. Every year, wherever she is, she sends me the money for my ticket and treats me to a holiday. I like it best when it's by the sea but sometimes it's in a town like Coventry or Sheffield. Didn't like Sheffield but beggars can't be choosers, I always say. I wonder where she is.' Lily looked around her as if Dixie might be concealed in Gwen's big, bright kitchen.

In spite of herself Gwen was electrified and asked as casually as she could, 'What exactly does Mrs Davey *do*, Mrs Beagerie? It must be some kind of job which entails a lot of travelling.'

The black sunglasses glinted at Gwen and Lily Beagerie gave another series of small coughs and then she said, 'My Doreen? She's a missionary, didn't she tell you?'

'A *missionary*.' Gwen's hand flew to her throat. 'No. No, she never said she was a *missionary*.'

Gwen sat down at the table, facing the old woman. She thought of the tiny black knickers she found drying on the radiator and the bottles of scent and expensive earrings on the dressing table.

'Surprised are you? Well, that's what she is; in the spring and summer she works wherever she's been sent to and in the winter she works at home. Writes a lot of letters, following up her mission and preparing the ground for next year.'

Warily, so as not to disturb her quarry, Gwen asked, '*Who* sends her, Mrs Beagerie? She doesn't seem to be attached to any particular church although she's been coming to the Bright Hour with me on Wednesdays.'

'She says it's the Lord Jesus. "Mother," she says, "the Lord Jesus is sending me to Bournemouth this year" – or it could be Oxford or Dundee – and off she goes. Done it for years.'

Gwen, watching the rings flash as Mrs Beagerie shakily lifted the cup to her mouth, felt a stab of conscience, thinking of the two sets of stairs the old woman would have to climb to her bedroom at the top of the house.

The smell of the cake cooking in the oven was sweet

and warm as they sat at the kitchen table. A clock which had once hung on the wall of Gwen's childhood home, a farmhouse high on the moors overlooking a valley scarred and scabbed with mine workings, ticked softly and heavily in the warmth of the kitchen, spear-shaped hands moving silently around the silver face. Lily Beagerie's head drooped and Gwen cleared away the cups and saucers as the older woman drowsed.

She wasn't quite asleep when they heard the front door opening. Lily Beagerie looked up at Gwen, who went into the passage that led to the front of the house. 'Mrs Davey,' she called, 'just a moment, Mrs Davey.'

Lily Beagerie pushed past her, tottering on her high, white heels. 'Hello, my duck.' She kissed Dixie Davey on both cheeks. 'Been working have you? I've had a cup of tea and a natter while I waited. Oh, I'm glad to see you.'

She linked her arm through her daughter's and together they walked upstairs. Gwen went back into the kitchen and started to peel potatoes for the evening meal; she had a lot to think about and to talk over with Ralph.

Under a window of yellow and sapphire glass where a small boat tossed on stormy waves while improbable rays of sun shone down on it, Lily Beagerie paused before starting to climb up steeper, narrower stairs to the two rooms that Dixie had negotiated with Gwen. There was a hand basin in each room but the lavatory was on the first floor, a fact not lost on Lily. She wanted to blame Gwen but knew from long experience that it would have been Dixie's parsimony that had relegated them to the attics.

The two rooms were neat and pretty, sloping ceilings being no disadvantage to someone as small as Lily Beagerie. Forget-me-nots dotted the walls, the blue repeated in curtains and counterpane. There were thick, soft towels and Gwen had filled a vase with a few early narcissi which scented the room with their sweetness. Lily slipped off her high heeled shoes and perched in the Lloyd Loom chair by the window.

There was a wide window seat under the sloping glass and she could see over the road and footpath, into the gardens of Jericho. Lily had lived all her life in the suburbs of south London and her interest in flowers and plants was limited. She *was* interested, however, in other people and watched with myopic curiosity two figures talking outside the largest of the glasshouses across the road. One she thought she recognised as Ralph Minto but the woman he was with was, as yet, unknown to her.

She was almost as tall as Ralph, slightly built, with hair so pale that it looked colourless in the fading light and a sideways way of listening that gave her a hesitant air. Her hands were deep in the pockets of an old tweed jacket and every now and again she would tuck a strand of straight, wayward hair behind her ear.

Lily turned to Dixie who had come silently into her mother's bedroom. 'Who's that with Mr Minto then?'

Dixie sat on the window seat and looked across the road.

'That's Binnie Seaton.' She turned to her mother. 'If you'd take off those awful glasses you wouldn't miss anything that's going on.' She looked out of the window again, watching the two figures in the dusk. 'Binnie Seaton owns the market garden and Ralph works there some of the time. Her husband died some months ago and I hear that she wants to sell up and move.'

Dixie smiled a little, thinking of the blue diary now locked inside one of her leather cases, and the pages that followed her underlined heading, BINNIE SEATON.

In the darkening garden, Binnie touched Ralph's arm and turned to walk back to the house. She had a straight backed, self-possessed way of moving and Lily watched her until she disappeared around a bend in the drive. Lily's judgements were as swift as they were capricious and she had decided at once that she didn't like Binnie Seaton.

Gwen, on the other hand, whose dislike of Dixie was understandable if uncharacteristic, found herself surprised at the amiable way in which she entertained her mother. Ralph was consulted about the times of trains to Truro and Plymouth and, when the weather was fine, Dixie Davey and her mother went out early after they had breakfasted together in the otherwise empty dining room. Dixie took only her usual cornflakes and toast while Lily Beagerie, who ate astonishingly well for such an old woman, relished the child-sized portions of scrambled eggs on toast or smoked haddock which Gwen enjoyed making for her, garnishing the little meals with parsley or tiny, cherry tomatoes.

Each morning of Lily Beagerie's visit brought its moment of astonishment: a dress the colour of Heinz tomato soup that made the old woman's skin look grey and drawn and for which she compensated with a circle of bright rouge on each cheek, or a nylon blouse so thin that a grey rigging of vest and petticoat straps could quite clearly be seen through it. Magenta and lime green, mauve and electric blue, all passed in a kaleidoscopic parade through Zion House and if Lily Beagerie discarded her hat, her candyfloss hair was covered in a pink chiffon scarf or occasionally, to Gwen's delight, by a snood scattered with artificial diamonds.

When Gwen had climbed the stairs to dust the two bedrooms and to put clean sheets on the beds, she was puzzled to find that there was no sign of the frivolities to which Dixie seemed accustomed, no jewellery, no lacy underwear lying around: only talcum powder and a hairbrush stood on the dressing table where before there had been rings and earrings and scent bottles. The two leather suitcases that Dixie had brought with her she kept in her bedroom, Ralph's offer to store them in an empty cupboard having been brusquely refused. Cautiously Gwen had tried the lid of the top case. It was locked and she was not surprised, sure that it concealed the objects usually displayed in Dixie's bedroom.

Gwen's candid disposition found it difficult to understand why Dixie Davey should deny her mother access to a side of her character that seemed freely available to others. Had Gwen guessed what else lay concealed in those locked cases, her somewhat ingenuous nature would have been dismayed for Gwen had lived her life by the uncomplicated precepts taught in the yellow varnished Sunday School in the Chapel on the moor.

Gwen's simple faith had comforted her through the days after the birth of her daughter, born tiny and too soon, who had died without Gwen being allowed to see her or to hold the little body. It had sustained her after her husband's early death, and now it formed the foundation of her life, habitual and unquestioned. Sometimes she wished she could persuade Ralph to come to Chapel with her, but on the occasions when he did, she remembered anew why she was glad that his visits were rare, for he fidgeted and sighed and cleaned his nails with a corner of the 'Parish Notices', snorting his censure of the Reverend Wilfred's sermon.

Binnie decided that before her mood of resolution left her, she would work her way through the disarray in the attics of Jericho. It had been warm enough for her to take her breakfast tea outside and she had sat on the mounting block beside the kitchen door noticing, without being aware of it, the early signs of spring; a discernable haze of green touching hedges and trees, sunshine intermittently slanting from behind clouds which were blown, fast and silently, across a pale blue sky.

She had stayed outside until she was chilled. The tea,

kept warm on the stove, was dark and bitter but she drank another mugful before gathering up boxes and large plastic bags from a disused pantry where she stored anything that she felt she might be able to re-use. Katha always laughed at her economies but Binnie still saw in her mind's eye Aunt Vee smoothing out brown paper and unknotting string and heard her aunt's gentle voice: 'It would take Uncle Basil a quarter of an hour to earn the money for this Binnie, so we really shouldn't waste it and it's sure to come in handy later on.'

All her life, Binnie had measured things in hours of Uncle Basil's time: it wasn't that she was ungenerous but her carefulness was inherent and it was this sense of guardianship – an unwillingness to diffuse further her separation from her parents – that had enabled her to refuse Richard's requests over the years to have Jericho and the market garden transferred to their joint ownership. Those people who saw Binnie only as Richard Seaton's quiet and acquiescent wife, knew nothing of the will power and strength of character that had enabled her to allow Richard to appear dominant in their marriage.

Binnie worked steadily, filling her boxes and labelling them, KEEP, OXFAM, JUMBLE. She tied tottering heaps of old *Horse and Hound* and *Country Life* into manageable bundles, resisting the temptation to sit and read, irritated by the dust floating and skittering around her. The telephone rang, barely audible at the top of the house, and she waited for Jory to answer it. It stopped after a long time and she remembered that she had promised to ring Katha, but decided that if she stopped working and went downstairs, she would find it hard to start again.

She moved pictures and broken chairs and old rugs into a sensible order, not having the energy to decide what to do with them, until only the cabin trunk and the boxes which had come from the vicarage remained, in a corner by themselves. The trunk was covered with labels of shipping lines that no longer existed, hotels that were hardly more than a memory, but it was one of the last links that Binnie had with her parents. It had been returned to England when they had been killed and although Aunt Vee had taken away anything she thought might distress Binnie, the trunk had been too good to discard and it had stayed in Binnie's bedroom. Each time it had been removed, Binnie had found it and dragged it back. She liked to sit on it, tracing the names of the hotels as if they were a talisman, while vignettes, enhanced by memory, of her father, so like Uncle Basil but jolly and laughing and smelling of cigar smoke, came into her mind.

Her mother, whose face she could no longer remember, was more of a feeling; a gentle disappointment still trickling through the years, of a daughter pale and plain, as if she had inherited the reverse of all her parents' robust qualities. Sometimes Binnie was guiltily aware of how lucky she was to have been brought up by an aunt and uncle who saw in her all that they had longed for in a child of their own and who were not astonished, as other people were, when Binnie had grown beautiful.

Her beauty was delicate: she was tall, almost too tall, but everything about her was graceful and she had a shy self-containment that could be difficult to penetrate: those who persevered discovered someone beguiling and merry and Binnie herself was quite unaware of the effect she had when she lowered her dark eyelashes over smoky topaz eyes. She had always thought of her eyes as being the wrong colour and had longed for them to be blue like Aunt Vee's.

When she could prevaricate no longer, Binnie opened the first of the boxes which she knew contained Uncle Basil's books. She hadn't wanted them at all but when the cold stone vicarage had been sold to a developer and

Aunt Vee was so confused, it had seemed easier to pack the books and take them to Jericho to sort through later on. 'Later on' had stretched into years and the boxes had stood in the attic, gradually acquiring a moleskin coat of grey dust which made her cough and settled on her hair and skin.

Apart from the books there was so little that had survived from her former life: Aunt Vee's silver hairbrush and photograph frame stood on Binnie's dressing table; a rocking chair which had stood in the vicarage kitchen now stood in the kitchen at Jericho but there was little else, the china and linen having been replaced long ago. Reluctantly, she scribbled JUMBLE on each of the boxes and turned to the trunk. Inside there was a tray which fitted across the space below the lid and Binnie lifted it off, using the cracked leather handles, one at each end. The tray was full of photographs and she put it to one side while she looked to see what else her aunt had put away.

She wasn't sure what to expect and wondered why she had never looked in the trunk before. Perhaps, she thought, it had been her Pandora's Box, but whether it was a fear of being disappointed at what it contained or fear of what she might find, Binnie didn't know. Now she felt a small frisson of apprehension as she looked into the bottom of the old portmanteau.

There were packages inside, wrapped in yellowy tissue paper and as Binnie unfolded the first one, the faintest fragrance of lavender brought her aunt so clearly into her mind that just for a moment, she imagined Aunt Vee standing beside her. In the biggest parcel was a knitted shawl, so fine and fragile that it looked like lace. Binnie had never seen one as beautiful and as she unfolded more tissue paper, tiny vests and pilches, bootees, coats and dresses appeared, all unworn and made with such love that it stretched across the years and enfolded Binnie in a ghostly embrace. As she disclosed each small garment, she put it on the wrappings which had hidden it, to keep it from the dust on the floor. When she had finished she saw that it was a complete, old-fashioned layette which had never been used and as she thought of her aunt and what her discovery meant, Binnie started to cry.

For the first time since Richard's death she cried as if her heart would break; for herself and her young, dead parents; for Jory who had never known them; but mostly for her aunt whose longing for a child had been so great and was now so pitiably tangible.

Dust clogged with tears on her cheeks and she couldn't breathe at all through her nose. She wiped her hands down the front of her shirt before re-wrapping each little piece of baby's clothing and putting it back exactly where it had been for so long.

There was a book which looked like a ledger at the bottom of the trunk and Binnie took it out. It seemed to be a diary in her aunt's handwriting so she put it with the photographs in an unused box to take downstairs with her. As she passed the study the telephone started to ring again and she put her box on Richard's desk while she answered it.

'Binnie?' Katha sounded out of breath. 'Where have you *been*, you said you'd ring. Anyway, I'll come over and we'll go out to lunch. About half an hour? Bye,' and Katha was gone without Binnie having spoken a word.

Binnie wasn't cheered at the prospect of seeing Katha. For some weeks there had been an awkwardness in their friendship and Binnie was always afraid that such difficulties were of her making. She was tired and dirty and she wanted only to make herself some toast and Marmite and to sit quietly in the kitchen and read, but

Katha in her usual headlong way had offered her no
choice so she went instead to shower and to change out
of her dusty clothes.

5

April

Binnie pulled the loose hairs out of her brush, curling them around her fingers before dropping them into the wastepaper basket. She concentrated on the sharp, black bristles and the lacquered handle, smooth as a pebble in her hand, so that she wouldn't have to look at Katha, to confront the disapproval she was sure she would see in Katha's dark, bright eyes.

Katha, sprawled on the bed, was chipping at her nails, unclean, ragged edges showing through the scarlet polish. She was watching Binnie drying her hair and as she turned her head, Katha noticed for the first time the wrinkles around Binnie's eyes and felt a little pulse of astonishment. Binnie had always looked the younger of the two and now she foreshadowed too clearly their middle age as she combed her pale gold hair into place, lifting each side with a tortoiseshell comb, her movements graceful and economical of effort.

Although the shower had refreshed her, Binnie's thoughts were still entangled in the past and she felt piqued that Katha had so unquestioningly assumed that she would be available. She looked up at Katha, a triptych reflected in the glass of her dressing table.

'Would you mind awfully if we didn't go out? I could make us an omelette here or there's bread and cheese, I think.'

Katha swung her legs round and sat on the edge of the bed.

'Honestly Binnie, you're becoming an absolute *hermit*; it'll do you good to come out for a change. Won't you? *Please.*'

Binnie knew that the surge of annoyance she felt was with herself, with what she perceived as her own weakness, not with Katha who would have given in to her, albeit with bad grace, if she had insisted on staying at home.

'As long as we go somewhere quiet then. I can't be bothered to make conversation today and you always meet so many people you know, Katha.'

Katha's laugh sounded rather too loud to Binnie, invading the pale spaces of her bedroom, filling her quiet world with vigour and life and colour. They had been friends for so long and still Binnie wondered sometimes what Katha saw in her. As children, Katha, small and stocky, Binnie, pale and thin, had been inseparable ever since Binnie, dressed in her new grey and blue uniform bought by Aunt Vee and much too large to allow for Binnie growing, had been rescued by Katha from mockery and ridicule.

They had grown up together, Katha's fierceness and quick temper moderating only a little; her forceful opinions directed now towards four daughters and a husband, who farmed the land where Richard had been hunting on the day he fell.

Rosmorran was large for a Cornish farm and, sheltered from the burning salt wind, Casey May ploughed around standing stones and planted his barley in fields where the stone hedges were almost as old as history.

Katha had seen him for the first time at the Royal Cornwall Show, his red hair making him conspicuous even if he hadn't stood a head taller than the tallest of his companions, and she had pursued him with all the singlemindedness that had attached her to Binnie when they had been eleven years old.

Katha was not as tall as Binnie and her sturdy body would before long start to thicken and her coarse black hair become mingled with grey. Her face already wore the expression of good humoured impatience that in time would harden into ferocity. Casey and their daughters had learned to navigate the storms of Katha's temper, for they never lasted long and were followed by the zephyr of laughter, all discord forgotten.

Binnie wished she had Katha's ability to say what she thought, to lose her temper and to recover her equilibrium with such ease, for Binnie seemed to the unobservant always to be the same, her pale beautiful face acquiescent and serene. Uncle Basil had discouraged displays of emotion and Aunt Vee had become so distressed if Binnie showed the darker side of her nature, that she had learned that it was better to hide her feelings with a smile; an eagerness to please replacing her own needs. It gave her the reputation of being good, while Katha was seen as headstrong and contrary. Aunt Vee had never entirely been won over by Katha and tolerated rather than encouraged the girls' friendship.

Binnie understood only vaguely that it was her steadfast nature, her belief in the truths taught her in childhood, that Katha relied on; Binnie's acceptance of the conventional, the antidote to Katha's recklessness. Neither could imagine being without the other and love and irritation held them together as closely as sisters.

They had been separated for the first time when they left school and during the year they spent apart, they wrote to each other every few weeks; Katha from Canada where she was helping her father's sister to look after twins born rather too late into a family already grown up, and Binnie from London where she was taking a secretarial course.

Binnie was at last living with the cousins she had thought might take her in when her parents had died, but now she wished with all her heart to be back in Cornwall. She found London frightening and dangerous, everything too immediate, too perilous for words, and when she had to return after the holidays to the crowds and the traffic-filled streets, she did so with no pleasure.

The cousins who had seemed so desirable from a distance never tried to hide from her that they found her dull, deriding her appearance as old-fashioned and out of date. Binnie shrank from confrontation with them, pretending to agree with their criticisms, disloyalty to Aunt Vee making her feel treacherous and impotent and sometimes she longed for Katha to come to her rescue again by silencing their teasing.

Sometimes her cousins insisted that Binnie went out with them, but she felt conspicuous and intercepted looks of amusement among their friends. She realised that she knew nothing of the things that interested them and she found their life threatening and frivolous. Binnie neither drank nor smoked and she found their attitude to casual sex difficult to reconcile with the façade of accepted behaviour with which they deceived their parents.

The Christmas parties had been particularly difficult to negotiate; groping, sticky hands and smoky breath trying to overwhelm Binnie's fastidious resistance. She went home to Cornwall for three weeks at Christmas and walked every day, glad of the rain and wind as if they could wash and scour away the dirt she felt was sticking to her body.

She had been afraid that she would have difficulty in concealing from Aunt Vee just how unhappy she was in

London but she was surprised that her aunt seemed to take her presence for granted, asking practically nothing about her work or her life away from the vicarage. There was, too, a hesitancy in her memory that concerned Binnie but when she tried to speak to Uncle Basil of her worries, he seemed evasive, always too busy to discuss them with her. Binnie wondered if it was just that three months' separation had brought into focus problems that had been there before she went away and which she just hadn't noticed, or whether something that she didn't understand was happening.

She wrote to Katha, but longed to be able to talk to her for Katha would have seen at once what was real and what Binnie was imagining. Katha's letters were amusing and, rather to Binnie's surprise, they arrived regularly all the time that Katha was away. Binnie always replied at once, long detailed accounts of her life in London. She never tried to hide from Katha her unhappiness or the dread with which she faced the next eight months away from Cornwall in that house full of pretence. She told her, too, that she was afraid that there was something wrong with Aunt Vee but that no one would talk to her about it.

After Christmas, Binnie had returned to London prepared for a travesty of spring away from the slopes of golden daffodils and the jewelled carpet of anemones which grew in the small sheltered fields above the bay. She was cheered to find snowdrops and crocus growing in great clumps in the London garden and waxy flowered japonica, drooping off its supporting trellis, thorns as sharp as needles. There were Lent lilies too, long neglected, turning their beautiful white heads to the ground, the pale pink tracery inside their petals hidden as if in shyness between hard, dark green leaves. Later there would be cherry blossom and bluebells, lilac and laburnum, all growing uncared for and wild in that garden where no one made time to look after them.

Binnie had rummaged in the garden shed and found a

few old tools among tins so rusty and bottles so cobweb-covered that it was impossible to see what they had once contained, and she had started to work in the garden. Her efforts made little impact but she was happier than she had been since leaving Cornwall and her cousins, after their first predictable reaction, lost interest in her and left her alone.

One day in the middle of that March, Binnie was in the garden, wrapped up against a wind which carried rain and which brought with it the sound of traffic from the main road. She had judged the ground too wet to dig and turned with pleasure to a task which she had been saving as a treat. There was a stone greyhound lying patiently with paws outstretched on the wall between the terrace and the grass, its head and right shoulder covered with lichen the colour of the sea in winter. Ivy had grown from the wall, curling and twining, making a regal collar of green and gold around the dog's thin neck.

Binnie worked carefully, revealing flanks weathered smooth and rounded by exposure; curious folded ears close to a wedge shaped head with the blue-green lichen like a splash of paint down the side exposed to the prevailing rain. She was removing tendrils, watching the tiny brown claws of the ivy ripping away from the stone, careful not to take away more than she need, when two young men came through the archway which linked the front and back of the house.

Binnie thought at first that it was her cousins returning and continued to smooth the soft curves now exposed on the little figure, not willing to be interrupted.

'Sorry to bother you, but there doesn't seem to be anyone in: we did try at the front door.'

Binnie looked up: two pairs of blue eyes, two neat haircuts, two pairs of very well polished shoes.

'We're looking for the Flinders – any of them really.

We're supposed to be going to a party tonight but we don't actually know where. I'm Richard Seaton.' The taller of the two held out his hand.

'I'm Binnie Carter, a Flinders cousin, but I don't know where they are. You could wait if you like and I'll make some tea.' She turned to the second young man. 'Oh! I thought for a moment that I knew you. Sorry.'

'Owles Court. Gymkhana. About ten years ago? Enys Williams,' and he, too, held out his hand, smiling at her.

And then Binnie remembered; remembered hobbling after Pippen, her little grey pony, nursing a collarbone broken in her fall before fainting into the arms of Katha's mother. It wasn't until the next day she heard that Richard Seaton had won the jumping, Enys Williams coming second. She felt herself blushing at the memory and looked down at the denuded greyhound, startled to see what an incongruously human expression it wore, congenial and somehow conspiratorial.

She had made tea for the three of them; there was no cake and the few biscuits left in the tin were broken into crumbs, so she made toast, thick slices swimming in butter. Richard and Enys, very easy with each other, drew her into their circle as if they were already allies.

'You had a very bossy friend, I remember. Kathryn? Kate?' Richard looked around and wiped his hands on the drying up cloth.

'Katha Easterby. She's still bossy and still my friend but she's in Canada for a year and I miss her.'

It was Enys who recognised the desolation in Binnie's voice and, wanting to help, he asked if she were going to the party.

'Oh, I hope not. I'm hopeless at parties but sometimes the Flinders all decide it's good for me to go. I don't know why they bother, I'd much rather stay here and read.' She pushed the plate of toast towards him but he shook his head.

'Quite, quite full, but Binnie *do* come. If you absolutely hate it, I'll bring you home, I promise.'

The two young men looked at each other and Richard added, 'We'll *both* bring you home, how's that?'

Binnie had gone to the party and sat with Enys on a spangled cushion until, true to their word, the two young men had brought her home, arms linked, singing in the cloudy spring night.

March turned into a blossom-filled April and April into a soft and gentle May. Binnie's dislike of London was tempered now by her own happiness. Richard and Enys seemed not to mind which of them she went out with, sometimes forming an affectionate and striking trio, Binnie tall and slender between the two young men, so unlike each other but each so handsome and orthodox amidst the long hair and flowing, glittery clothes that were everywhere.

Enys was sent to Berlin in early May so it was Richard who was with Binnie when Katha's mother telephoned to tell her that Uncle Basil was dead.

'Binnie darling, he didn't suffer at all, just dropped dead on Sunday morning after Matins. Snuffed it, just like that.' Mrs Easterby sounded exactly like Katha but Binnie wondered why it wasn't Aunt Vee talking to her.

Richard had been so kind, putting her on the train at Paddington with magazines and a box of chocolates. Just like an old film, Binnie thought. She had been feeling odd even before Mrs Easterby had telephoned and she blamed the chocolates, her favourite rose and violet creams, for the waves of nausea that made the journey so uncomfortable.

Mrs Easterby had met her at Penzance, her car reeking of old dogs, and Binnie had closed her eyes and dug her nails into the palms of her hands in an effort not to be sick, the smell almost overwhelming her.

'Binnie darling,' Molly Easterby called everyone 'darling'; 'Binnie darling, there's something I've got to tell you.' Binnie opened her eyes trying not to breathe too deeply. 'It's about your aunt: it's quite ghastly but dear old Vee's almost gaga – hardly knows that poor Basil's gone and I'm afraid that she may not even recognise you, my pet.'

Six weeks later, in the last week of July and half an hour before a thunderstorm broke over London, Richard and Binnie had been married. After the ceremony, to which no one had been invited except two acquaintances of Richard's to be their witnesses, he had taken her back to the tiny house behind Brompton Oratory that he shared with Enys and Henry. Enys was still in Berlin and Henry was walking in France, so they had it to themselves while Richard worked out his notice.

Binnie was just twenty-one, pregnant and very rich. She felt chastened by the contempt that she saw in her cousins' faces and no one had been sorry when she moved her clothes and books into Richard's house. The space she had occupied in their lives closed over behind her like a neatly mended tear.

Binnie didn't think that she was in love with Richard and she was sure that he wasn't in love with her but he wanted to marry her and Binnie, too familiar with submission, could see no reason to refuse him. If Enys intruded on their thoughts neither of them mentioned it apart from in the most superficial way. He wrote from Berlin wishing them every happiness in the world and for the first time in her life Binnie was glad that he and Katha were so far away.

Richard took her down to Owles Court to stay with James until they could find somewhere of their own to live. Richard had very little money, apart from what he had earned, and he seemed quite happy when Binnie suggested that she might buy a house for them. She had been hesitant in suggesting it and was surprised at the alacrity with which he accepted her offer. She wondered if Richard had been hoping that James would ask them to live at Owles Court but James, although hospitable and kind, knew well enough that his life would not be so pleasurable if he had to share it with his younger brother.

They had found Jericho almost at once, intrigued by the name on the agents' particulars. It was a square, grey house, considerably too big for two people, but Richard was delighted with it and saw his plan for a market garden coming to fruition without the need for a great deal of persuasion. The fields that had surrounded Jericho Farm until a hundred years ago had been built over, granite terraces covering pasture and crops, some larger houses and a few small shops where cottages had stood and cattle had grazed.

It was August when Binnie and Richard stood looking at the garden, three acres of neglected lawn and flower beds, the kitchen garden rampant with seed heads. The front boundary of Jericho Farm had been moved when the footpath had been made linking Trewavas Terrace with the main road into town and the rose garden, now separated from the rest of the property, was in danger of becoming a public area, the tall iron gate forced sideways and hanging off its hinges while there were signs of people using the neglected garden as a park.

The railings which had surmounted the low wall of granite slabs now resembled rusty spears abandoned after a battle. There had been pressure to remove the railings as a danger to children but as no one could be found to take responsibility for the garden, the railings were still there, more dangerous for being hidden, sharp and corroded, in hedges of briar rose and privet.

Richard and Binnie had walked around the house,

pleased with its solidity. Two granite pillars stood beside the front door, grey twisted trunks of wisteria half-encircling them.

'Needs pruning,' Binnie murmured, letting the dry, faded tassels fall into her hand. There was a conservatory at the side of the house, peeling white paint and broken windows a raffish highlight to its intrinsic elegance. They forced the door and went inside, their feet crunching on a scattering of glass, before walking across grass so starred with wild flowers that it looked like a meadow.

'It reminds me of *Les Cocquelicots*,' said Richard. 'What do you think Binnie?'

Binnie stood still, seeing in her mind's eye the deep borders filled with silver and white and dusky pink. She would make a herb garden near the back of the house and plant pot marigolds and rosemary and lovage. 'No stables – would that matter?'

'No horses.' Richard's face wore a curiously childlike expression as if he were at a birthday party and had just realised that everything he liked best was on the table and he could have something of everything he wanted.

While Binnie had been working in the attics, the day had grown warm and sunny. By the time she and Katha got to the Adelaide she was mollified a little at the disruption to her plans. Several people were already there enjoying the sunshine and Binnie chose a wooden bench far enough away from them to prevent peripherally overlapping conversations. Katha put a glass of orange juice in front of her and sat down holding a double gin.

'Food's coming. I ordered large pasties, they're scrummy here, almost as good as home-made. Well, *better* than my home-made actually.' She laughed and again it sounded too loud, too boisterous, and Binnie waited for Katha to tell her what was wrong, lethargy settling around her like a cloak.

At a table to their right she was aware of the handsome blonde woman who was staying at Zion House and she supposed that the tiny woman with her was her mother; Ralph had told her about them although she hadn't taken much notice at the time. As she sipped her juice a dark figure sidled through the opening which led to the garden from the back door of the pub. Doddy Rowe collected the glasses left on the tables and pouring all the dregs into one, he went to sit on the wall, putting his hand to his greasy quiff as he passed Binnie. He wedged himself between two upright stones and drank his repellant cocktail with every appearance of enjoyment.

Sadie Clements followed Doddy into the garden, carrying a tray on which sat two golden pasties big enough to feed a working man, paper napkins, salt and pepper but no cutlery: knives and forks were for visitors who left their pasties on the plate and cut them into pieces.

'Gosh, they're *huge*, Sadie. I'll never manage all that.'

'Well if you can't, I know someone who'll be glad to finish it up for you.' She nodded in the direction of Doddy Rowe. 'Poor old devil, he's a proper nuisance but you can't help feeling sorry for him although most of it's of his own making.' She put their plates on the table. 'Those Rowe brothers are as bad as each another but at least Doddy isn't nasty like that Jos – just can't keep his hands off other peoples' property, that's all.'

Sadie had worked in the kitchens of The Adelaide for years, saving enough money each summer to pay for a holiday in the late autumn when the visitors had all but gone and prices came down. She and Charlo had been all over Europe and this year she had started her job earlier than usual as they wanted to go to San Francisco. Like many Cornish families, they both had cousins in America whom they had never met, descendants of Cornishmen and women who had gone out to the goldfields and who had never returned home. She put the tray down and sat on the end of the bench.

'They can spare me for five minutes.' She looked at Binnie, wanting to say something about Richard, wanting to talk to her about Jassy and Jory but hesitant about broaching the reserve of the other woman. She liked Binnie, acknowledging someone as strong as herself, and Binnie saw beneath the chatter and laughter that always surrounded Sadie a core of common sense and kindness and a belief as firm as her own in traditional virtue.

'The love birds had a good time last night I gather.' She glanced at Katha and explained, 'Jory and Jassy – courting strong they are.' The three women laughed together and Sadie, encouraged, went on in her softly accented voice, 'She's a little monkey, that one; good job Jory's going to Dartmouth, he's such a lovely boy I don't want him to be hurt and I'm afraid that my Jassy will break a few hearts before she settles down.' Sadie thought fondly of Jassy whose bright little mind absorbed everything so easily and just as easily released it before passing on to something more interesting still.

'I always hope that Jory will pick one of my girls, goodness knows there's enough to choose from. I don't mind which one really, but I think Dinah's got her eye on him so she might give Jassy a run for her money.' Katha looked amused and Binnie thought that if Dinah had inherited her mother's tenacity, then Jory would have no chance. Sadie stood up, then sat down again, her accent becoming more pronounced as she became animated. 'You'll never guess who I saw earlier. Do you remember that Enys Williams who was friendly with Richard and James years ago? It was him, I'm sure; I can remember him when we were all small and he lived at Tiverton Villa with his grandparents.' She turned to Binnie; 'He used to stay with the Seatons later on, didn't he?'

'He was at school with them,' Binnie said. 'James was a bit older, of course, but Enys and Richard were always friends. I met up with him again in London before Richard and I were married but I haven't seen him for, oh, twenty years I suppose. James has mentioned that Enys visits him from time to time so I expect that when you saw him, Sadie, he was staying at Owles Court.'

She held her pasty in both hands and bit off the corner, the sweetness of the turnip and the smell of the onions making her suddenly ravenous. She was aware of the blonde woman listening to Sadie's cheerful voice as she walked away, her feet as sure and pretty as a goat's on the rough slab path.

Sadie was a big woman with a body as soft as dough. Her size never hampered her and she was full of energy, even her thick, silver hair seemed to have a life of its own and her brown eyes encouraged confidences, confidences which were never betrayed however much she chattered. She had a habit of touching someone on the arm and saying, 'Now, I'm going to tell you something,' and sooner or later gales of laughter would follow her revelations. Everyone liked Sadie but there were those who underestimated her.

When Sadie had gone back into the pub Binnie looked over the curve of the bay: it was like half a bowl in which someone had washed out a paintbrush, green and mauve and inky water swirling together in a translucent patchwork. Buildings rimmed the middle of the bowl and beyond them were fields rising gently in corded stripes or spring-soft green and there were still some neat splashes of daffodil yellow on the lower slopes. The town grew upwards from the harbour; a dry dock and a swing bridge stood near a sloping quay and here, when the tide was out, men in waders and barefooted boys dug for lugworms in the shining black silt.

Binnie could see it all in miniature from where she sat in

the garden of the Adelaide, opal light softening the outline of St Michael's Mount where it swam in the ruffled sea. The sun was strong enough to reflect off the water and from windows of buildings on the higher ground. The church where Richard's funeral had been held stood on the highest hill of all and there was a grand theatrical cupola over a bank near the old Market Hall. These two buildings seemed to dominate the town which grouped around them, tall and grey or with brilliantly whitewashed walls; palm trees and hydrangeas crowding every street and garden in the summer. Much nearer, there were sun-bleached clothes drying on lines hauled high above back yards on supports as tall as flagpoles and everywhere there were gulls, hard bright eyes always looking for an opportunity to scavenge and steal.

While she had been looking over walls and yards, envied domestic enclosures of other peoples' lives, Binnie had been eating steadily, content to sit in silence in the warm air and the pure, bright light that even in winter was hardly diminished. She was used to Katha's moods but wondered why they had come to this garden away from her familiar kitchen and why Katha was drinking double gins in the middle of the day. Suddenly she put down the remains of her pasty.

'I know there's something wrong, Katha, can't you tell me what it is?' she asked. 'Is it Casey – or one of the girls?' It often was one of the girls and Binnie had sometimes thought of the oddity of life where someone as fierce and implacable as Katha had been given four daughters while she had only one son.

Katha was looking at her empty glass. 'It's not the girls this time and it's not Casey either; well, not exactly.'

Binnie waited, conscious that the woman from Zion House was trying to hear what they were saying, the lenses of her sunglasses glinting like petrol on water as she glanced in their direction.

'I know you think that Casey's wonderful, putting up with me and my temper all these years but, oh Binnie! he's so *boring*. He could bore for England and I can't stand it.'

'You mean he's suddenly *become* boring?'

'Of course not and it hasn't mattered much up 'til now, but . . .' Katha stopped and Binnie, understanding something quite suddenly, said, 'You mean that Casey's shortcomings are annoying you now that you don't have Richard around to alleviate your boredom.' Her voice was cold.

'Oh don't go all "Musings from a Cornish Vicarage" on me Binnie, I couldn't bear it and, yes, I *do* miss Richard but it's not what you think – you can't believe I'm *that* awful.'

Binnie picked a few crumbs off her plate and threw them to the sparrows which hopped, quite unafraid, around their feet. She didn't know what to say, unwilling to relinquish her isolation, to be caught up once again in the turbulence that Katha generated.

'Here goes then.' Katha tilted her glass in case a drop or two of gin had gathered in the bottom, 'I'm having a little fling and I need you to give me an alibi.'

Binnie thought of Casey who worked as hard, harder, than any of the men he employed to give Katha and their daughters the sort of life that Katha accepted as their due. Binnie had seen the look behind Casey's eyes, ardent and amused and loving, and she had so longed for someone to look at her like that. Casey made her laugh; the merry being inside Binnie responded to his gentle humour, two quiet people who understood each other very well. Binnie knew that she had a *tendresse* for Casey but it was something she always found hard to acknowledge even to herself, a fondness for someone else's husband.

Whatever Binnie wanted to say to Katha remained unsaid as Katha went on, 'You must help me Binnie; if Casey rings, won't you just tell him I've been with you? I know it's awful of me but really it's no one you'd know and Casey'd be so *hurt* if he found out.'

Katha demanded so much of Binnie, but she asked her for very little and Binnie had never learned how to refuse her. Katha's face was beseeching but Binnie could see the beginning of a small, satisfied smile around her mouth, certain that Binnie would comply in the long run, the pattern of their friendship set years before when she had given her patronage and Binnie had accepted the subordinate role.

Perhaps it was Katha's assumption that Binnie would do as she asked or the presumption of shared guilt, but suddenly Binnie felt the resentment that sometimes engulfs the outwardly docile, and she put her glass down on the table with a thump.

'No Katha, I won't. Not now or ever again. I've told enough lies for you and I won't help you to deceive Casey.' Binnie's hands were shaking and she could feel her lips tight across her teeth.

Katha looked at her, ready to bully and plead but seeing how close Binnie was to tears, she pushed away her plate saying quietly, 'Well, I can't say I blame you. I shouldn't have asked but I thought you'd do it for Casey's sake.'

'No you didn't Katha, you thought I'd do it for *your* sake and don't pretend even to yourself that you didn't. What you're doing to Casey is no different from what Richard did to me and I can't believe that you don't understand that.'

Katha looked at Binnie and said, 'I suppose Pinocchio won't help?'

'Not any more.' Pinocchio had been their childish code word when either had lied to protect the other. 'We're too old for Pinocchio; too old altogether.' Binnie picked up her shoulder bag and slid along the bench. 'I'll walk home Katha, I've rather a headache. Will you ring me?'

Katha nodded, her eyes small and too bright, the smile gone before it had even surfaced. She let Binnie walk a little way down the hill before going into the pub to pay for their lunch.

As soon as she had driven off in her big black Rover, Doddy Rowe heaved himself off the wall and went to the table where the two women had been sitting. He put the leftover bits of pasty into a paper napkin and was back perched on the wall when Sadie came out to clear the tables. She handed him a pint of beer.

'Mrs May's compliments – go handsome with that pasty you've got.' She laughed and pattered away, leaving him to listen to the conversation between Dixie Davey and her mother while he dined on unforeseen bounty.

It had been an enthralling hour for Dixie and she was anxious to get back to Zion House. She thought with pleasure of opening her locked suitcase; of taking out the big, blue diary, selecting the red pen to underline a new heading – KATHA MAY.

Lily Beagerie was watching her daughter's face, shielded from the bright spring sunshine as was her own, by dark glasses. Dixie's hands were rolling a paper napkin into a tube, a fan, a boat; big, ugly hands with flat, undistinguished nails. Lily thought of the other times when those hands took on a life of their own; letters pouring off an assembly line, manufactured by hands which designed and constructed threats and hints, produced as easily as a machinist might produce a screw with a spiral thread.

'Doreen, my duck,'

'Dixie, Mother. I've told you it's Dixie.'

Lily continued as if she hadn't heard, 'Doreen, why don't you stop before there's any more trouble? I like it here, better than anywhere we've been before and I've been thinking.' Lily's hands were folded together on the table, the beautiful rings heavy on hands that looked like little claws. 'I'd like to stay here for a bit, perhaps even for good. Mrs Minto told me that sometimes the whole winter goes by without any frost, think of that, and hardly ever any snow.'

'Do be sensible Mother, it rains for weeks on end and the wind blows a hurricane half the time. Anyway, you'd soon be bored without your friends.'

'I've got no friends Doreen, you know that *and* you know why.'

Dixie's hands worked frantically, pleating and smoothing her napkin.

'Why don't you get a proper job, duck; I could sell the house and buy a nice little place down here. I'm sure it would be better for you and I think I'd like to stay in one place, I'm getting a bit too old for all the gallivanting.'

'What would we live on then? You know what always happens when I get a job.'

And Lily did know what always happened. Dixie, so confident and smart would have no difficulty at the interview, her secretarial skills impeccable; her manner, if somewhat intimidating, engendering confidence in her capabilities. All would be well for a few months and then the woman for whom she worked – it was always a woman, Dixie would never work for a man – began to notice that letters which had never been seen by her were answered and filed away; she heard of advice which had been given over the telephone and which she knew had not emanated from her; decisions required, professional judgements sought, all delivered themselves into Dixie's hands – and went no further.

Investigations were made and reprimands followed; Dixie would work on for a little while in the job for which she had been engaged and Lily would hear daily complaints of 'how *can* I be expected to work for a woman like that who knows no more than I do'. When the complaints began to include the vulgarity and offensively ostentatious lifestyle that Dixie had to witness and endure, Lily knew that only the next stage, that of a whispering campaign to detract from Dixie's credibility, remained between her and unemployment.

It was when Dixie was working for a solicitor that the idea grew upon her that there were many people, troubled people, who would benefit from having their lives focused and directed by someone with a mission to help them. She had gathered a great deal of information from the files before she was, inevitably, once more dismissed, but Dixie was exultant; she had found her true calling and jubilantly she began her life as a missionary.

New friends sometimes found it difficult to imagine Dixie as a married woman but she *had* been married, for ten years to a man who sold agricultural machinery. It was not his chosen profession, but a stopgap which had expanded to fill his life at a time when he found it agreeable to be away from Dixie for days at a time. They had been introduced at a Conservative Party New Year dance and he had immediately been attracted and amused by her self-assurance although it never for a minute misled him into thinking that she was anything other than an ambitious girl from a suburb on the wrong side of the river.

Dixie may have been brought up in south London but she was determined not to stay there and she had learned quickly from the women for whom she had worked. Her voice underwent a renaissance and she learned to buy one real leather belt or one silk scarf instead of two or three in synthetic materials. She had pretty hair, thick and honey blonde and she soon learned to save up and go once every six weeks to the same hairdresser as her employer for a good cut, harassing a neighbour into giving her cheap highlights and demiwaves the rest of the time.

She had no real talents except those which promoted her upward path nor any pretension towards the intellectual although she said that she adored music and certainly had a 'Highlights of Chopin' tape which she played softly in the background at her twice-yearly sherry parties. She read books only when they were condensed in *Reader's Digest* and neither appreciated art nor realised her deficiency. No one had more acquaintances than Dixie; everyone she met was a potential friend and she was welcomed everywhere but she was always the first to leave any gathering, before her presence palled. Her sense of timing helped to conceal the shallow nature of her character, friendships shifting and changing with every new introduction.

When any of her friends were down on their luck or unhappily in love, Dixie was the perfect companion, sympathetic and supportive in turn, but when the crisis was averted, the gloom dispelled, Dixie lost interest and became remote, intent on helping someone else whose anguish she shed as lightly in its turn. This was particularly true where troubles of the heart were resolved by a man. Then Dixie would withdraw her support almost coldly, with warnings about the irresolute and spineless iniquity of all men.

Throughout the ten years of her marriage and despite having shed all other connections with south London, Dixie continued to spend time with her mother. Once a week she would take her to the supermarket and watch the profligacy with which Lily filled her basket with white bread and processed peas, air fresheners, bright cakes, frying steak and out of season tomatoes. Dixie did her own shopping late on Saturday afternoon when the store reduced everything that had reached its sell-by date. Her husband became accustomed to a disconcerting medley of yoghurt and cream cakes and pulpy, dying fruit. If Dixie bought meat, it was always the cheapest cuts which she never learned to cook properly, her slight interest in food being governed only by how little she could spend on it. Her favourite meal which she had every night when her husband was away selling his machinery, was a boiled egg and half an orange. She was never tempted to eat the whole orange.

It was not altogether surprising, therefore, when her husband, while staying in a boarding house somewhere near Rye run by a widow who gave him fried bread and bacon and made pastry as light as his mother's, wondered audibly about leaving Dixie. Dixie declared that she couldn't live with a man who had committed adultery in his heart and moved back to her mother's house telling her husband that he would have to wait five years for a divorce.

At the end of five years Dixie's husband and the widow had two little boys and were running a private hotel in Eastbourne and Dixie had begun her life in the fertile mission fields that lay, with covert opportunity, wherever she felt obliged to go.

For the first year of her mission she had felt that she was called to Bournemouth and she had found a job as a relief night receptionist at a large hotel on the seafront. It was out of season when Dixie had started to work there, businessmen and conference delegates making up most of the clientele before the hotel became busy for the summer. There were parties of tourists too: large, candid Americans with complaining, always exhausted wives, and it was here that Dixie learned to watch and remember and where friendly sympathy and a guileless willingness to listen, provided her with all the armaments she needed for the winter months when her work to help relieve the conscience of her erstwhile confidants began.

After several year's experience perfecting her technique,

Dixie began to counsel directly some of those she knew to be troubled and a hint so faint as to be almost imperceptible, of difficulty in paying her rent or finding the train fare to visit her mother, was almost always rewarded with a donation to the mission. Two principles applied to all Dixie's work: she was never immoderately greedy and she knew when to stop.

Soon Dixie no longer had to look for work to finance her mission. She spent the summer in guest houses or small hotels, becoming so much an accepted face in her own small territory that barriers which were never penetrated by the usual visitor became doorways through which Dixie passed and from within which she found those in need only too ready to pay for redemption and willing to contribute to her mission in exchange for the satisfaction of absolution.

Doddy Rowe heaved himself off the wall where he had been spinning out his pint for as long as he judged his presence would be countenanced and shambled past the table where the two women were still sitting.

Lily seemed unaware that they were the only people left in the garden of the Adelaide and started to talk again, determined to pursue her argument. 'I don't want to live on the proceeds of blackmail any more, my duck, because that's what it is: no matter how you dress it up talking about missionary work and the Lord Jesus' plans for you, it's blackmail, and sooner or later you'll be caught.' Her face became still as she thought back to a time when a friendly new neighbour, a social worker with the local council, had started asking questions that Lily found difficult to answer. It was after Dixie had been asked to leave yet another job and she had been in one of her excitable, irresponsible moods, throwing out hints like torn paper, almost as if she were laying a trail to her discovery. Lily had avoided the girl's overtures although she was a nice little thing and to her relief Dixie said that the Lord Jesus had found her work at a conference hotel in Peterborough. When Dixie had come home to spend the winter months capitalising on her carefully acquired knowledge the neighbour had moved on, but the apprehension of discovery had never left Lily.

Since she had been staying at Zion House, something in Lily Beagerie had changed. She had come to understand and gradually to accept that by condoning Dixie's extortion she was implicated as surely as if she had written the letters herself. Dixie's compulsion, which furnished them with such a comfortable living, had become a burden from which Lily longed to be free. She wanted to live as other people lived, uneventful lives filled only with commonplace activities; lingering over shopping and meeting friends for coffee, gossiping in the kitchen and acquaintances to acknowledge her as she walked along the windy promenade to buy her quarters of fudge. She was determined to do all she could to achieve her desired end and now she looked directly at Dixie and said again, 'I don't want to live on the proceeds of blackmail any more, duck. I've always gone along with it because I've been afraid of what would happen to you if someone turned nasty, but I'm tired, Doreen, tired of it all and I want you to stop.' She hesitated and then said softly, 'I want you to stop and if you don't, well, I'll have to *make* you – and I can you know, have you ever thought about that?'

6

May

Enys Williams arrived at Zion House in the late afternoon, parking his car under a street light as he would have done in London. It had been an easy drive, too early in the year for the roads to be congested and frustrating, and he had enjoyed watching the scenery change as he drove almost from east to west of the country.

Sheep grazing in neat, garden-like orchards, tidily hedged, had given way to acres of wheat and barley just greening the land while fluorescent yellow diverted his eyes. He loved the cheerful colour, not thinking it a blight and an eyesore any more than the blue-green of cabbages or rosy coloured shoots of new hawthorn in the hedges.

He was in no hurry and had kept off the motorway, taking the slower, quiet roads, anticipating his pleasure at arriving where he wanted to be, by the sea. As he drove from east to west the look of the houses had changed, from white-painted clapboard to red brick to golden hamstone and finally to grey as he drew nearer to Cornwall.

In Somerset, Enys had turned off the road to rest beside a river where silver fingers of willow would stir the hot still air in summer and where now bare yellow wands of new growth shone in the eclipsed light. There was a little broken bridge, unsupported spars tumbling down the bank towards dark water, deeply shadowed but hiding the iridescence of a rainbow. Kingcups grew on the bank and soft pink and green leaf buds were opening on an alder stump.

Enys knew he was happier than he had been for a long time and threw small sticks into the slowly running river, watching until they caught on the roots of a tree. He had been where pain and illness had become so entwined that he could no longer distinguish one from the other but Eloise had gone and he had slowly surfaced through layers of self doubt and misery until he could now accept that she no longer loved him. He wondered if he had ever really loved her, and he knew certainly that he had. She had been so gay, so full of vitality, pulling him after her in all her enjoyment of life. He, so unquestioning, so English, had been happy to settle into the secure routine of married life leaving Eloise stranded in boredom on the shore of his contentment but it had been Enys who had left in the end, packing only what he needed into a suitcase and a leatherbound grip, a note left for Eloise to find when she came home, softer and sweeter for a while, from the bed of one of her lovers.

Enys had gone to his stepfather's house in Plymouth and that kind, unquestioning man had given him an anchorage until he was well again; Enys' mother, busy and happy at her coffee mornings and bridge afternoons and theatre evenings, never took seriously her son's difficulty in adjusting to life with his vision of the future occluded by failure.

'Darling, you're so clever and so handsome you'll soon find someone else, but you won't do it by sitting at home all day listening to that dreary music. Come to Margery's with me, her niece from Australia's staying with her and she's full of fun, just what you need.' She wheedled a little, 'Just to please me?'

Enys had gone with his mother and Margery's Australian niece had played with him like a huge, uncontrolled puppy with an old sock, leaving him exhausted and depressed. His mother continued for a little while to encourage him to socialise but eventually she grew exasperated with his obstinacy and it was his stepfather, remembering perhaps the small boy he had first seen watching the world from the green shadows of his grandparents' garden, who encouraged in Enys an interest in antiques, taking him to auctions and country house sales where they bought books and drinking glasses which they dispersed covertly around the house, prodigal conspirators in their enjoyment of the old and elegant.

Enys had divorced Eloise, giving her everything she wanted, anxious to relinquish the tangible reminders of failure, that the failure wasn't his he couldn't accept. He had gone back to London, to a rented flat and to the shreds of the life they had shared. He was well again but deeply unhappy, and when James Seaton wrote asking him to come and stay at Owles Court for a while he had shut up the flat and gone without a second thought. At school, and as young men in London, Richard had been Enys' friend but he was fond of James and had stayed with him from time to time over the years, James almost perversely concealing their friendship from his brother.

During that holiday at Owles Court, on a windless summer day when the smell of decomposing seaweed was hanging heavily in the air, he had gone to see the house where his grandparents had lived. Tiverton Villa was twice as big as the terraced houses which it adjoined but from which it was detached, only half of it standing in the Terrace, the side elevation facing the main road which ran between the town and the sea. It was surrounded on three sides by a wall of pebbledash which stretched on its longest side to meet the wall in the back lane, little empty sockets of sandy mortar showing where small fingers had plucked and scrabbled at the shiny little stones over the years. There was a monkey puzzle tree in the middle of the grass on the right-hand side as you looked at it from the road; to the left, a tree fern, its trunk covered with coarse black hairs like some old, recumbent animal. There were no flowers or intrusive coloured shrubs to disturb the harmony of the garden and even the sun, which shone so brightly on Trewavas Terrace, seemed hesitant to insinuate itself into the shaded, fern-dark charm of Tiverton Villa.

Enys had stood by the wall of the house where he had spent his first remembered years, overwhelmed by almost physical melancholy as he thought of the time he had spent there, smothered by his grandparents, protected by them from contamination, while his mother, young and pretty and a widow, seemed so seldom to be with him. He remembered lying in bed listening for the absence of silence which meant that she was home, and going to sleep on so many nights in the silence that isolated his grandparents in anxiety and complacency like the glass in the bathroom door, covered with scrolls and whorls designed to obscure from the curious the person inside.

When his mother had married again and they had escaped to Plymouth to be near his stepfather's work, the feeling that now surrounded Enys was something that he slowly came to recognise as happiness. He loved his stepfather who introduced him as 'my boy Enys' and who deflected his mother's quick anger with a kiss and a hug. For the first Christmas that they spent as a family his stepfather had given Enys a ship in a bottle that his father had made and given to him and even now it still brought Enys joy and reassurance.

*   *   *

When Enys had returned to Owles Court later that day, he had entertained James with his story of being kidnapped by Pearl Angove the minister's wife, and being obliged to use all his powers of dissimulation to avoid answering her questions.

'She remembered me you know, James, from all those years ago; said it was my funny Williams' hair, would you believe.'

Enys himself saw nothing remarkable about his hair: he had begun to go grey while he was still at school and by the time he was in his early twenties he had thick, straight silver hair that people remembered long after they had forgotten his handsome, sharp-boned face or the sweetness of his smile.

James had laughed with him: it was one of James' greatest gifts, that he was able to make anyone feel a lot cleverer and more amusing than they really were and in his company Enys was unwinding and becoming restored. James was always pleased when a friend took an interest in the garden and together they subdued the rhododendrons which were colonising the wood behind the house, sawing and chopping and dragging branches to pyres near the compost bins, James resting several times while Enys worked on alone.

When Enys had stayed at Owles Court on previous occasions James would tell him how Richard and Binnie were, how Jory was growing, in a matter of fact way unembellished with detail, but now, with Richard dead, it was as if James needed to talk about his brother, recalling for Enys, as they sat over their whisky and water in the evenings, shared incidents from long ago. Did he remember the year they started an archaeological dig in one of the fields high on the cliff, or the time when they lost the oars of the dinghy and drifted round the headland before beaching on a strip of shingle in the dark?

'I thought we'd be drowned for sure but Richard wasn't afraid,' Enys said, 'he was much braver and always better than either of us at everything. He was even better at being ill: do you remember the Easter holidays when we all had mumps and lay on the terrace in those old steamer chairs, like patients in a sanatorium? Richard was much sicker than either you or me but it was the only time I can remember him being ill at all.'

James lay back in his chair, whisky glass held in both hands. 'He should have had all this really, he'd have been much better than me at looking after the estate and I could have spent my time pottering about with my books and papers.'

'That's nonsense, James, and you know it. If Owles Court had gone to Richard it would probably be a conference centre or a country club by now or the park would be a golf course and you'd be living in the stables over a tea room and gift shop. He couldn't handle money at all, never could. It would have been a disaster.'

James was quiet for a long time, then he said, 'It's going to Jory you know. I've told Binnie, so that she's free to do whatever she wants with Jericho.' Enys said nothing and James went on, 'I suppose, you see, Richard was so used to having his own way in everything that when he found in Binnie someone who wouldn't give in to him, he really didn't know what to do. He treated her very shabbily you know; very shabbily and she didn't deserve it, poor little thing.' He drank his whisky in one long pull, not looking at Enys. 'I couldn't help much but I hope that she finds some happiness now.' He held out his hand for Enys' glass but Enys shook his head.

'You've always been a good friend to her, James, and now she relies on you a good deal I suspect.'

'Yes, I accept that but I don't know how much longer I'm going to be of any use to her. You know the Jewish saying, do you, "Take what you want says God, and pay for it?" Well, in my case the debt has been called in.'

It was as if the air in the room had suddenly stopped moving. Enys had known James too long to offer him the solace of hypocritical disbelief but the unexpected casualness with which James spoke of his condition had shaken him. Two small strokes that James had suffered a year ago had been, the doctor said, a warning, and James, although not yet middle aged, must not take for granted continuing good health.

'Time for our walk I think, before I get maudlin. I wanted you to see the *magnolia stellata*, it's at its best in this dusky light.' James opened the French windows and they stepped out into the soft evening air. The magnolia's slender white petals looked lustrous in the twilight; it seemed so fragile but was hardy enough to bloom in the earliest days of spring. James could see that Enys shared his pleasure, a pleasure that until a few months ago he would have taken for granted. He let one of the lovely flowers settle in his hands for a moment before they turned back towards the house and their usual excellent dinner.

Gwen had been anticipating Enys' arrival since mid-afternoon, a tray set for tea on the kitchen table was waiting only for her to pour boiling water into the lustre teapot when he arrived. The teapot was a particular favourite of hers, gold and magenta flowers wreathed around the fat, fluted sides, a small chip on the spout its only flaw. Black trees with orange fruits circled the cup and saucer and rimmed the plate which held her home-made shortbread. The china was part of a broken set that Gwen had bought at an auction and she thought it pleasing, unaware of its value to a collector.

Once or twice she had gone to the windows at the front of the house to see if she could see Enys. It was the dead time in the middle of the afternoon and the silence of the streets was heavy and familiar. Preparations for dinner were finished; it was too early to turn on the television and Gwen would have liked to rest but she didn't want to be full of sleep when he arrived. Sometimes she felt more tired than she would admit to Ralph, afraid to burden him with any sign of ageing, intent on remaining his friend and collaborator for as long as she possibly could.

The second time she had looked out, she had seen Cora Neville walking home with Hannah, the girl's dark hair blown against her face as they turned the corner. She walked with her feet turned in towards one another and Cora had to slow her pace but did so without any sign of impatience. There was no one Gwen didn't recognise and she sat down to wait, taking her knitting out of a flowered bag which she kept beside the sofa. She was making Ralph a jersey for his birthday, and the dark green wool and intricate cable pattern which she had used so many times before flowed competently from her hands.

At four o'clock Gwen stopped knitting and made herself a cup of tea. She heard Lily Beagerie and Dixie Davey come in and go upstairs just before five and then, at last, there was a ring on the bell and Enys Williams was there, standing in the enclosed front porch, red and gold and blue diamonds of coloured light dressing him in Harlequin's clothes.

Gwen had Pearl Angove's description of him in her mind's eye. 'Tallish, grey hair, big nose, not bad looking really if you like that stand-offish kind', but even allowing for Pearl's sparing generosity, Gwen was startled to see how handsome Enys was. His thick silver hair gave him the look of a young man playing the part of someone much older and he had eyes so dark a blue that they were like faded denim. When he smiled his sweet smile at her, as he did at once holding out his hand, Gwen felt flustered and disconcerted and heard herself speaking too fast and too effusively.

'Do come in Mr Williams, I've been expecting you. Did you have a good journey? Were the roads awful? I expect you'd like some tea but I'll show you your room first. Please come this way.'

Gwen led the way to the bedroom on the first floor, directly underneath the rooms occupied by Dixie Davey and her mother and overlooking the long frontage of Jericho. Enys put down his case and went at once to the window. He could see glasshouses behind the hedge, his imagination conjuring Binnie and Richard out of the shadows as they had been when he had last seen them, imagining the unknown Jory still as a small, sturdy boy with the confidence of his invincibility still whole and strong in him. As he watched, a man came out of the gate, crossed the road and was lost in the shadow of the house directly underneath Enys' window.

'My son Ralph.' Gwen was standing by Enys; she had nearly recovered her composure. 'He works at the market garden when he isn't helping me here but I don't know how much longer he'll be able to do that as it's being sold, I believe.'

'So I understand.'

Gwen looked at Enys in surprise, then remembering what Pearl had told her, 'Of course, you know the Seatons don't you? Well, just Binnie now, of course. Oh, and James. I'd forgotten that you used to live here. At Tiverton Villa wasn't it?' Enys nodded and Gwen went on, 'We were all so sorry about Richard, he was so young to die like that. Ralph has helped Binnie as much as he can but she seems determined to move and I can't say I blame her, it's such a big house and Jory'll be going away soon and then she'll be all on her own there. Not that Richard seemed to spend a lot of time at home, too busy gadding about and up to no good a lot of the time.' Gwen stopped. 'I shouldn't talk so much. Take no notice of me Mr Williams, I'll go and get your tea.' She put the key to the front door on Enys' bedside table and left him to unpack and to think about what she had said.

Enys put away his clothes in the tall mahogany press and looked around his room. He was greatly amused by what he saw: there were several rather good engravings on the walls, every one of them slightly foxed and every piece of china bearing a small chip or crack. The tall, swivel glass was so misty that his reflection reminded him of an ageing actress photographed through gauze. It was all unexpectedly charming but he was glad to discover that Gwen's passion for rescuing the old and damaged didn't extend to his bed. The duvet was soft and the mattress just hard enough; there were plenty of thick towels and extra pillows were on a shelf in the wardrobe. He thought he would be very comfortable in Zion House and he liked his plump, seemingly indiscreet landlady although he had a feeling that her chatter was less ingenuous than she would have him believe. He went downstairs in a happily expectant mood, wondering if Gwen had been trying in a roundabout way to tell him something.

She was listening for him and took the tray into the guests' lounge when she heard Enys coming downstairs. Ralph had helped himself to a piece of the shortbread and too late she noticed the space and crumbs on the plate. Enys smiled at her again and Gwen put the tray down, turning away from him so that he wouldn't see the confusion in her face. She went back into the kitchen where Ralph was reading the newspaper. He glanced at her and then looked again more carefully at his mother's face. She seemed to peep at him from the corner of her eye and there was an unfamiliar expression on her face.

'Mr Williams has arrived.'

'I know. I tried his shortbread.'

'So you did.' Ralph waited for a reprimand but Gwen walked towards the pantry, stopping just as she went in to say, 'I should think he could cause a lot of trouble with a smile like that,' and from inside the cupboard Ralph heard, 'I only wish I was twenty years younger.'

'Why, Mother, I'm shocked.' Ralph looked at her fondly, secure in the certainty that no one, certainly not a man as young as himself, would deflect Gwen from her chosen widowhood, it suited her too well: Ralph always available to mend and paint and move furniture; no one to question how she spent her money, no one to undermine her decisions. No, she was happy as she was and Ralph, too, saw no reason to change their way of life.

Change was coming though, he knew that, and he was at that moment looking through the estate agents' particulars in the newspaper to see if Jericho was already being advertised for sale. He hoped whoever bought it would keep him on as he didn't really know what else he could do, a life spent entirely at Zion House was too claustrophobic to contemplate. Binnie had said that James Seaton might be able to find work for him but in the meantime Ralph was busy keeping Jericho in good order so that it could be sold as a going concern.

Binnie seemed to have no plans other than to move and said vaguely that she would perhaps stay at Owles Court for a time, while she decided what to do. It occurred briefly to Ralph to wonder if the arrival of Enys Williams would encroach in any way on Binnie's plans, but he dwelt only momentarily on that idea, as one of many that passed through his mind as he tried to put his thoughts in order.

There was nothing in the paper about Jericho and Ralph decided to go and talk to Charlo Clements. As he stepped into the back lane he saw Enys Williams walking slowly down Trewavas Terrace towards Jericho. Ralph had no doubt who it was from the description Pearl had given to his mother and he decided against going into the Clements' house by the back door as he usually did and decided instead to follow Enys around to the front, watching him until he turned the corner of the road and walked towards the promenade.

As Ralph passed the Nevilles' house he saw a curl of blue smoke in the recess of the window. He smiled towards the unseen Cora and raised a hand: he liked Cora Neville and Hannah too, careful and patient with her, willing her to flourish as he did his plants.

The Clements' kitchen was less than half the size of the one at Zion House and it always seemed to be overflowing. The Clements children and their friends formed changing tableaux accompanied by the hum of a washing machine constantly in use and at least one radio always piercingly audible. The telephone ringing, quarrels, laughter and Sadie singing in her beautiful contralto voice tugged at Ralph. He was always glad to visit the Clements, absorbed tacitly into the fabric of their lives – and glad to go home again to quietness and ironed shirts and dinner eaten sitting down, listening to the goings-on in Ambridge which ran like a thread alongside his own. Ralph and Gwen thought of the Archers as friends and discussed their lives over the evening meal, sorry that Phil was becoming curmudgeonly and glad that Jill was finding the spirit to answer back to dreadful Lynda Snell.

The Clements' house was uncharacteristically quiet when Ralph rang the bell. Charlo, shoeless, in grey socks, let him in.

'Talk of the devil,' he said, 'Sadie and I were just wondering what you'd do when Jericho's sold.'

'You've heard then?'

Charlo laughed. 'How long do you think something like

that could be kept quiet? Of course we've heard, heard all sorts of rumours too. You must know what's going to happen to it, if anyone does.'

'It's on the market, that's all I know. As a matter of fact I thought it would be in the paper today but I couldn't see anything.'

Sadie came into the sitting room with three mugs of coffee on a tray and dropped down into a corner of the sofa.

'How're you my handsome?' She leaned over and gave Ralph a kiss on the cheek. 'Isn't it lovely and quiet – don't know where any of the children are but I expect they'll be back when they're hungry. I'm tired out, busy old day at the pub, first really warm day and everyone was out in the sun. Saw Binnie and Katha at lunch time, and that blonde woman staying with you. If you ask me she's as odd as all-get-out.' Sadie reached for her mug and looked at Charlo. 'Have you told Ralph what we were talking about just now?'

Charlo looked at her, exasperation fighting with affection in his face. 'If you'd give me a chance to get a word in, I might.'

Sadie said an unconvincing, 'Sorry,' and began to sing quietly as Charlo turned to Ralph.

'We were just wondering how much Jericho will go for. Whether we could possibly afford to buy it.'

Ralph tried not to look overtly surprised but Sadie saw the expression on his face.

'I've always loved it, you know. I used to play in the garden when I was a little girl but I knew I'd never live anywhere like that but now, well I don't know, Charlo and I reckon we could run it as a business. I could do B and B and Charlo could keep the market garden going and I could cook all fresh food and build up a restaurant side. What d'you think Ralph?' Sadie put her hand on her husband's arm. '*We* both think we could do it, don't we Charlo?'

Charlo looked at Ralph. 'Yes we do, but the drawback, as usual, is money. You've *no* idea how much Binnie wants for it?'

Ralph shook his head. 'No idea at all, but we should hear soon.' He sat thinking for a minute and then said, 'You'd keep the market garden going Charlo? Perhaps I could stay on there, I know how everything works after all.' He didn't notice the flicker of a look between Charlo and Sadie as their carefully scattered seed found a fertile resting place.

They continued to gossip gently, Sadie making them laugh with her story of Doddy Rowe's pasty lunch and Ralph telling the Clements of Enys Williams' arrival.

'Funny little soul he was,' said Sadie, 'sometimes he would come home with me, and my dear old mum would give him milk and cake or apples, whatever we had in, and he'd gobble it up as if he hadn't eaten for a week. I reckon those old grandparents of his never gave him enough to eat but he'd have been in trouble if they'd found out he'd been home with me, not good enough for the likes of the Williams, I wasn't.' Sadie shook with laughter. 'Do you know what we called his grandmother? "The Witch". We did, she looked just like one and I always thought Enys might be changed into a white mouse or something.'

'You do talk some rubbish Sadie.' Charlo was laughing at her again. 'Right enough though; I was scared stiff of old man Williams, he always seemed to be around the corner when you were doing something you shouldn't and he'd go straight off and tell your parents. Reckon Enys had a hard time until his mother married that sailor and they went away – Plymouth, wasn't it Sadie?'

'Somewhere up-along anyway. I wonder why he's come back.'

Ralph was comfortably settled on the sofa. He enjoyed listening to the Clements talking of their childhood. They had grown up together in this same small town and knew most people by sight, a lot of them as friends or acquaintances.

'I believe he wants to buy a house down here. Haven't met him yet but I've seen him.' He looked down at his big, clean hands and said, 'Mother's very taken with him anyhow. Said she wished she was twenty years younger, what d'you think of that!'

Enys had walked past Jericho on his way to the sea. Everything was as he remembered it, the Big House of his childhood where he went to tea at Christmas, his grandparents giving him butterless bread and jam before he left home in case he ate too much and drew attention to himself. Once he had pushed two pink iced buns up the front of his best grey jersey and in the games that followed tea, crumbs had trickled out and the icing had stuck to his shirt in a soft, damp wodge. Someone had taken him away and cleaned him up, someone with soft, white hands and a gentle voice who smelled as sweet as the icing on the cakes.

It was at one of those Christmas parties that Enys had first met the Seaton brothers. He was a little afraid of Richard who won prizes in nearly every game and became noisy and a nuisance when he lost. James, two years older and quieter, sat and talked to a dark haired young woman whom Enys recognised by her smell as his erstwhile comforter. Mrs Seaton had asked Enys to visit them at Owles Court and, surprisingly for such a timid child, Enys quickly learned to ride well and he discovered that Richard was not so fearsome as he had thought.

They were friends all through their schooldays at Lamborough and Enys spent nearly as much time at

Owles Court in the holidays as he did with his mother and stepfather. James had gone on to Oxford and Richard to share a tiny mews house near Brompton Oratory with a friend called Henry Hopcroft, and here it was that Enys kept his books and belongings and where he slept when he was in London.

Binnie Carter and her friend Katha Easterby rode at Owles Court gymkhanas, the girls as disparate in character as were Richard and Enys, but just as close friends. Katha and Richard were always the leaders, Binnie and Enys usually happy to follow them.

When Enys and Richard had met Binnie in London just by chance when they were looking for her cousins, the Flinders, it had seemed as if only weeks had passed, not years; years in which they had all grown up and Binnie had changed from the pale, plain child they remembered into a self-contained and beautiful young woman. Both young men were captivated by her and the rivalry which had always lain under the surface of their friendship was now exposed, no less fierce for being politely and jocularly acknowledged. It was Richard, of course, Richard who had to win all the prizes at a party, who won the biggest prize of all and Binnie Carter became Binnie Seaton while Enys was on a tour of duty in Berlin.

Enys thought of all this as he walked towards Newlyn on his first evening in Cornwall on what he thought of as the start of his new life. The sun was a half globe of fiery scarlet as it sank into inky dark water, the air was almost cold and the fronds of the palm trees rustled as they brushed against each other in the constant breeze off the sea. Enys knew there was a restaurant a little way along the road where he would be able to sit in the window and watch the lights come on from one end to the other in the horseshoe of the bay, while he ate whatever fresh fish had been landed at Newlyn that morning.

He was content, sure now of the rightness of his return. His search for a house would begin in the morning and then he would go and see Binnie and, perhaps, meet Jory for the first time.

7

May

Binnie heard nothing from Katha for several days. She thought a great deal about their conversation at the Adelaide and wondered if she had been too harsh, Uncle Basil had always impressed on her that she should not judge other people. 'Love the sinner but not the sin,' he had said but Binnie knew quite surely that what Katha was doing was wrong. Binnie wondered if she would feel any different were there not at the back of her mind the dichotomy of her own feelings for Casey. She was afraid that her refusal to compromise her conscience might lead to a greater harm being done and she was as sure as she could be that Katha would not have been deflected from her chosen path by the withholding of any help.

She tried to imagine what would have happened had their roles been reversed. Would Katha have lied for her? She knew that Katha would have done so if she could have been sure that no one would discover her in the lie. If there was any danger of detection then Katha would have refused, laughing it off, no lingering doubts at all in her mind. Katha's sense of self-preservation was greater even than her loyalty to Binnie. Binnie wished she could have made light of the situation but it was not in her nature to do so, adultery seemed to her to be so very wrong. She had never been able to agree that sins of the flesh were small in comparison with sins of the spirit, too many years of the inadvertent learning of secrets at St Euny's vicarage and far too many years of living with Richard had taught her that lies and deception and even theft were so much part of an adulterous association that it was not one sin but a composite of many: and that it *was* a sin she had no doubt.

She had never understood how anyone, even Richard who mocked her vicarage morality and teased her and tried to convince her that human weakness was not a sin as she believed, couldn't see that the pain which almost inevitably followed for someone innocent, outweighed a transient pleasure. She couldn't be light hearted about it, feeling again the anguish of the betrayal of her trust in Richard whenever she heard of an affair between people she knew, and always counterpoint to her censure was the knowledge that her own child had been conceived before she was married.

No one had seemed to find it remarkable that her marriage to Richard had been so quiet. If anyone thought about it at all, the suitability of a quiet marriage in London seemed *convenable* as her uncle had just died and her aunt was obviously ill. Perhaps only Katha's mother might have guessed the truth but Mollie Easterby was so busy sidestepping scandal on her own account that she didn't dwell on the probabilities of Binnie's situation.

It hadn't really occurred to Binnie that Richard might be unfaithful to her, her view of life formed as it was by the code that supported life in the vicarage where such behaviour would have been unthinkable: words like 'fornication' and 'adultery', biblical and uncompromising in their bleakness, coming into her mind when she heard others laughing about someone's unfaithfulness, a feeling almost of revulsion swamping her common sense at the thought that someone sitting at her table, eating food she had cooked, was engaged in an adulterous affair. Binnie's good manners allowed her superficially to continue to treat the friendship with her usual pleasant commitment but trust had been lost and Binnie never again depended on the word of someone she perceived as untrustworthy. She was intelligent enough to wonder sometimes if her conviction in some absolutes was wrong, an unquestioning belief the easy option.

This unconditional disapproval of the failure of other people to live up to her own strict moral code, caused Binnie much heart searching in the months following Richard's death. She came reluctantly to accept that Richard had been seen to be human, excuses for his behaviour being easily sanctioned in the face of her perceived self-righteousness. Stories of his exploits became exaggerated, part of the folklore of the circle in which they lived, and sympathy for Binnie became sporadic. Only those closest to her took care not to hurt her further by showing that they thought her attitude extreme, Katha disputing fiercely any suggestion that Binnie was somehow to blame.

And now Binnie had refused to help Katha and she felt wretched and sanctimonious, doubts about the sincerity of long held beliefs surfacing in an uncomfortable and protracted conflict in her mind. She decided to go and see Katha and to try to put things right between them.

Rosmorran lay equidistant from the north and south coast, in the narrowest part of the peninsula which formed Land's End. Rough croft land surrounded it, spoil tips sparsely covered. It was land where it was wise to tread carefully for there were many old workings, concealed by brambles and ferns and golden gorse, invisible and dangerous. A river, a tributary to the much larger river which ran into the sea at Hayle, ran through Rosmorran land, giving it water meadows of lush, green grass where the cattle of earlier years had given way to Casey May's horses.

The farm settled snugly into the green valley, bypassed by main roads and almost hidden from the harsh, scarred landscape that was all that most people saw as they hurried through it to the sea. Casey's father had bought Rosmorran after the war and it was one of the few farms in the area which wasn't owned by the Duchy. The farmhouse itself had been built much earlier in the shelter of the valley sides. It was square and grey like a house in a child's drawing. A porch with coloured glass protected the front door from any wind and a large window on either side of the door and four more windows in a row on the upper storey balanced its plain frontage. A garden in front of the house was surrounded by a wall of interlocking stones, like those which quartered the farm and which Casey refused to break down to make it easier for the farm machinery to move between fields. The garden was ragged grass and shrubs; there was no time to spend on growing flowers, generations of annuals seeding themselves with vivid abandonment wherever they could. A row of staddle stones marked the left hand boundary of a makeshift tennis court. No one used the front door and the porch was full of faded deck chairs and pots of dried up geraniums with desiccated brown leaves, dusty and forlorn and woven with spiders' webs.

Rosmorran was large and comfortable. Katha, in spite of her impatience with domestic chores, was a natural homemaker and a wonderful cook. This often seemed to surprise people, who mistook the disorder of the household for indifference. Even Binnie, after so many years of friendship with Katha, could still be shocked by the filth encrusting the mixer or the casual way in which Katha washed up the dogs' bowls with her own dishes.

A girl called Cherry Eva came in every day to iron and ostensibly to clean the house but she was just as likely to help in schooling one of the horses or to be found swimming with the Mays' daughters in the heated, covered pool while the pile of ironing never seemed to diminish and was the catalyst for many of the arguments that racked the household.

Cherry's father worked a small farm on the high ground above Rosmorran and had found a fleeting fame amongst other local farmers by saying loudly in a royal presence that he would rather put dynamite down his drains than hand back to the Duchy the farm he had worked on all his life. Cherry was a blithe big girl, reliable and conscientious and always willing to cover up for any of the May girls – except Dinah. Cherry had been in love with Casey May from the day she arrived to work at Rosmorran but was pragmatically courting one of his workmen.

Dinah, to whom Cherry Eva felt such uncharacteristic antagonism, was the only one of the four girls who took after Katha. She was sturdy, with abundant dark hair and a temper that flared and crackled with impatience. She was younger than Hester, older than Mary and Grace, all of whom resembled their tall, red-haired father, but it was Dinah whom Casey was hoping would follow him onto the farm, having accepted that there would now be no son for him and Katha.

Casey took the girls to Mass with him every Sunday, Katha sometimes going with them at Christmas and Easter but refusing even to consider becoming a Catholic herself. She had never made it difficult for Casey to practise his religion, preferring to disregard it as she might a time-consuming and esoteric hobby. She was able to ignore most of the teachings of the Church but as her daughters matured she made sure they understood that a pregnancy caused by passion was one thing but one caused by the Pope's teaching on birth control was quite another. They were a formidable, argumentative family, Casey an oasis of quiet among the five women, whom he loved and for whom he worked so hard.

Casey had never liked Richard Seaton a great deal, perceiving him as superficial and untrustworthy where most others saw only charm. Richard had kept two horses at livery at Rosmorran and Casey had been intending to ask Binnie what she wanted to do with Navaho, the young grey gelding that Richard had been bringing on to replace Drummer, his old hunter. Drummer had been destroyed after the fall in which Richard had died and Navaho needed to be ridden. Casey was thinking about the horses when he saw Binnie's car drive into the yard and park near the loose boxes. Katha was out and Casey had a feeling that there was some difficulty unresolved between her and Binnie. He walked to the back door.

'Lovely to see you Binnie, are you well?'

'Fine thanks, Casey. Is Katha in? I should have 'phoned really.'

'Katha's not here, nor are the girls and nor, so it seems, is Cherry. Just me – will I do at all?'

They had moved into the kitchen and Binnie tried to hide her astonishment at the disarray that was everywhere. Casey saw her expression and laughed.

'Terrible isn't it? You'd think squatters lived here wouldn't you, not five grown women. I'd offer you coffee but I don't suppose there's a clean mug in the house.'

Binnie was hesitant about interfering in someone else's kitchen but she looked around for the kettle and plugged it in, clearing a space among plates of stale food and stacks of yellowing newspapers. She found two mugs, saw that Casey was rummaging for instant coffee in a cupboard that seemed to be full of sticky jars, and suddenly she felt angry. She slammed the wet mugs onto the table, the drying up cloth too filthy to use.

'What's going on Casey? Where the hell is Katha?' As soon as she had spoken the words, she regretted saying them, hanging like something tangible between them in the desolation of the kitchen. Casey looked at her and she could see shadows that looked sooty on the white skin under his eyes.

'I was going to ask you about Navaho, eating his head off out there,' he nodded towards the yard, 'but perhaps that's not the question I should be asking you.' Casey put two large spoonfuls of coffee into the wet mugs and Binnie poured water into them, her hand shaking. 'You don't know where Katha is either then?'

Binnie shook her head, wishing she had not come; wishing now that she had agreed to give Katha her alibi to save Casey from hurt. Her breath was uneven as she tried to make her voice sound reassuring. 'Perhaps she's gone to see me and we crossed each other on the way. She did say something the other day about wanting to talk to Jory.' She glanced at Casey again, trying to convince herself that she was telling the truth so that he would believe her.

Casey moved a pile of clothes from the kitchen table and sat across the corner, his uncommon height seeming to telescope so that he was facing Binnie directly. She looked straight into his eyes, noticing a flaw she had never seen before: it was as if a black tear had slid from the pupil and carved a path through the slate blue iris. His golden eyelashes were very long.

'You're not much of a liar, Binnie.' He pulled a handkerchief from his pocket and found a patch that wasn't covered in oil on which to blow his nose. 'I don't know what's gone wrong this time but I'm afraid it may be serious.'

'You mean Katha's ill, I didn't realise. I'm sorry Casey.'

'Katha's not ill; sick of me perhaps, but not ill.' Casey looked at Binnie, waiting to hear her ask what he meant but she said nothing and he spoke again. 'How long have you known each other? Nearly thirty years isn't it and you don't know what I'm talking about do you?' He didn't seem angry but his voice sounded tired. 'For most of the time we've been married Katha has had what she calls 'little' affairs, but this time something seems to have gone wrong and I'm afraid she may have got herself into something she can't handle.' He waved an arm at the mess surrounding them and half smiled at Binnie. 'It's never been as bad as this before.'

In the silence Binnie could hear a fly buzzing, trapped and frantic in some sticky, curdled mess. She felt tears pricking her eyes and put a hand down to the table to steady herself. She tried to speak but her voice didn't seem to work so she drank a mouthful of dreadful coffee and tried again. 'You mean that she's done this before?'

'Lord, yes. You know about this one then? I felt there was some trouble between you two but I didn't think Katha would involve you in her little flings. Shows that she must be troubled, knowing how you feel about – well, things of this sort.'

Tears were running down Binnie's cheeks as if they had an independent life over which she had no control. Casey pulled out the filthy handkerchief again but put it away and reached out to wipe Binnie's face with his big, hard hand.

'It hasn't made a lot of difference to us you know. I'm a dull sort of a fella and Katha has so much energy.' Casey was trying to be diverting, to smooth the look of hurt from Binnie's face. 'It wasn't like Richard, Binnie, honestly. Katha's always been discreet, never anyone we'd be likely to meet and it's never lasted long.'

'Oh Casey, she doesn't think that you know, she doesn't want to hurt you, for you to feel betrayed.'

'Ah well now Binnie, betrayal's not a word I'd use. She's never betrayed me in her mind you see.' He stopped and said quietly, 'Until now, that is.'

Binnie was still trying to understand what Casey was telling her. 'But don't you *mind* Casey?'

'Of course I mind and I mind more as the years go by but I've always pretended that I didn't know, it was better for all of us that way and I couldn't have kept Katha if I'd tried to change her. You should understand that, surely.'

Binnie shook her head. 'I don't believe I could ever really have loved Richard, not the way you love Katha.' She started to cry again and Casey put his sinewy, sunbrowned arms around her and pulled her against his shoulder. He smelled of sweat and oil and something sweet, hay or cattlecake. The sleeves of his shirt were rolled up and Binnie knew that above the material his arms would be white. Farmers' arms, she thought, and wondered what she was doing in this squalid kitchen, being held so closely by her best friend's husband. She stopped crying and looked up at him. Casey's skin looked tight, his nose too prominent, the sooty shadows under his eyes like a bruise. Binnie touched them very gently and Casey bent his head and kissed her. She tasted her own tears on his mouth and the fan of his long, soft eyelashes on her cheek made Binnie remember things she had thought never to feel again. A longing for someone to hold her and kiss her again and again changed into a feeling that frightened her and she pulled away from Casey, gulping as if the air between them was too thin for her to breathe. Casey's face was whiter than ever. 'God, Binnie I'm sorry. I didn't mean . . .'

She interrupted him. 'It's all right. It's all right. Just a mistake. We both made a mistake. It won't happen again.' Binnie was speaking in small jerky sentences as if she needed to breathe more than usual, like a climber on a mountain higher than the one for which he had prepared himself.

Casey stood up, his height isolating him once more. 'Still friends Binnie?'

'Oh Casey, of course. What would I do without you and Katha.' She stopped as if Katha's name had acquired a new, eclectic meaning between them. 'About Navaho,' she tried to sound like the Binnie of an hour ago, 'if you'd like him for one of the girls, please have him. You could look on it as payment for all the months you've had to feed him. I don't suppose Richard ever did pay you regularly, did he?'

Casey put his hands in his pockets and looked down, not willing to acknowledge that Richard had hardly ever paid him and that he was too generous to press him, knowing that it would be Binnie's money used to settle the debt.

'I thought not. I'm sorry Casey, I should have done something about it before this.'

'An awful lot of apologies around here today.' Casey looked better, some colour in his face under the brown, outdoor skin.

'There's a lot I'm sorry for Casey; more than you'll ever know, I suspect.' Binnie picked up her car keys, hesitating, uncertain how to leave. 'Ask Katha to get in touch, will you?' She was unwilling to go without trying to help him. 'I think it'll be all right you know.' Binnie tried to sound reassuring. 'Katha's always been a bit, well, giddy.' Aunt Vee's funny, old-fashioned word came into her mind, 'But she's very sensible underneath, much more so than me but you'd have to know us well to understand that. She's very honest you see, doesn't try to hide things like most people do: a bit uncomfortable sometimes but perhaps it's better in the long run, no skeletons to fall out of cupboards.' Binnie forced herself to smile a bright, detached, social smile at Casey, the longing to feel his arms around her again pushed deep down where it would be buried by duty and commonsense and the acceptance that it was wrong and that she was culpable. She left the kitchen without giving Casey the usual peck on the cheek and drove home not sure if it was tears or drizzle on the windscreen that made the journey so difficult.

Lily Beagerie was sitting in the kitchen at Zion House watching Gwen make crème caramel for the next day's dinner. Enys Williams had said that he would like to eat in and Gwen thought she might learn a little more about his business if he relaxed over a good meal.

In the morning she would collect the sweet local lamb chops she had ordered and the first of the new potatoes were in the shops; clear chicken soup and her special crème caramel to finish with. Gwen felt inhibited from trying foreign recipes, Ralph and most of her visitors liked plain English cooking and this she did very well, using the best ingredients and taking care not to overwhelm the food with what she saw as unnecessary embellishment. She particularly liked making cakes and profoundly enjoyed watching the disparate elements meld into a perfectly risen, aromatic whole. Gwen's cakes were a work of art and Lily Beagerie often appeared at the kitchen door at tea time, Gwen having found no mannerly way to resist the intrusion.

Gwen was watching the sugared water darken to caramel, leaning over the saucepan to smell the exact moment when she would need to turn off the cooker and pour the boiling liquid into the fluted glass bowl she always used.

'A lot of work in that. Why don't you use a packet mix, they're just as good.' Lily was watching Gwen as she made the custard, straining it into the bowl on top of the caramel before very gently sliding it all into the oven in a baking tin half full of water.

'I'll save you some tomorrow and you can see what you

think.' Gwen smiled at the old woman and saw that Lily was looking tired although she had done everything she could to counteract that impression. She was wearing a pink blouse with a white Peter Pan collar and puffed sleeves that looked as if it had been made for a ten-year-old girl; her pleated skirt was of an incompatible pink and the travesty of the resemblance to a child was enhanced by Lily's shoes. These were of black patent leather with an ankle strap like those worn by a girl in a Norman Rockwell painting, that innocent image disfigured by chunky, high heels which gave Lily her characteristic tottering walk.

In an effort to add colour and vivacity to her face Lily had put on a necklace of beads that looked like partly sucked fruit gums, with earrings so heavy that they dragged down her thin, old earlobes. She took off her sunglasses and laid them on the table. Gwen, looking sideways at her, was touched by the old woman in her brave, bright clothes. 'You'll have a cup of tea, Mrs Beagerie, and there's still some saffron cake, you enjoyed that didn't you?'

'I enjoy everything you make and I like it here better than anywhere else we've been. Do you know what I like best?'

Gwen shook her head, cutting two slices of bright yellow cake speckled with lemon peel and currants.

'I like the palm trees, I do. Makes it seem very foreign. And the people and the sea, and most of all I like the little kiddies on the beach with their lollies and buckets and spades before they want those buzzy earphones and computer games and start making a nuisance of themselves. Oh, thank you duck.' Lily broke off small pieces of cake and lifted them to her mouth as if she were feeding someone else, a child perhaps. Gwen sat down next to her, glad to rest her legs. 'I want to stay here Mrs Minto.' Gwen looked up. 'Not *here* I don't mean, but I'm trying to persuade Doreen to look for a house we could buy; I think it would do her good to settle down.'

'But what about her work Mrs Beagerie? I thought Mrs Davey had to travel to different places. Didn't you say that she could be sent anywhere?'

Lily Beagerie was pressing yellow crumbs together on her plate and was silent for a long time. Gwen knew better than to hurry her and waited quietly. At last Lily looked up. 'I want Doreen to change her job too. I've never been happy with this missionary lark, it's too dangerous.'

Gwen wondered for a moment if perhaps Lily Beagerie was confusing Dixie's work in the tranquil towns of England with something she had seen on television; Palestine perhaps, or Belfast. 'Dangerous, Mrs Beagerie?' She spoke cautiously, 'More cake?'

'No, ta but I wouldn't say no to another cuppa.' She pushed her cup towards Gwen. 'Oh yes, it's dangerous work all right.' She started one of her crackling laughs and Gwen felt uncomfortable as if she were the butt of a joke which she only half understood. Lily Beagerie's laugh ended with her usual cough. 'Better for me too, this sea air. I've got no friends you see, not up there, Doreen doesn't encourage it, but I feel I've made friends down here and I want to stay.'

She sounded defiant but looked dry and shrivelled like an old leaf and Gwen put her warm hand on the old woman's arm. Under the child's puffed sleeve the flesh was grey and skinny, dappled with the brown marks of age.

'We usually close in the winter to spruce the place up; we do a bit of painting and Ralph shampoos the carpets while I wash the curtains. I don't think I could take a permanent guest but you might get a long let quite cheaply once the season's over. What does Mrs Davey think?'

'We don't need to *rent* anywhere: I've got a place to sell in London and we could buy a nice little house down here. The problem is that my Doreen likes to keep on the move.'

They heard the front door open and Lily Beagerie stood up. 'Thanks for the tea, Mrs M. I'd better be going, won't do for Doreen to find me gossiping.' She stood like a wizened child to put on her sunglasses before turning to Gwen. 'I'm an old nuisance aren't I?'

Gwen smiled her sweet, soft smile; the smile of a mediator, a peacemaker. 'Of course not my dear, you can talk to me whenever you like.' Lily Beagerie wavered out on her high, misleading shoes and Gwen turned off the oven and lifted out a pudding cooked to creamy perfection.

It wasn't after all Dixie Davey coming in that the two woman had heard: it was Enys Williams. Three of the houses he had looked at that day he had dismissed at once. One was detached as he had specified, but next door to a busy garage which didn't show in the estate agent's contrived photograph. Another, like an overdressed guest at a party, stood forlorn and embarrassed on the edge of an estate of bright, uniform bungalows; and the third had an atmosphere that made Enys feel uncomfortable, a participator at some secret ritual. He had made his inspection and hurried away.

He wasn't discouraged, indeed he was enjoying the freedom of access to the small, hidden vagaries of strangers' lives. He had stopped for lunch at a pub called The Lamb and Flag and while he waited for his smoked mackerel he shuffled the estate agents' particulars in front of him in an effort to sort the misleading from the realistic. The landlord of the Lamb and Flag was a big man whose flesh seemed to have slid downwards on its frame, leaving a small head stranded over a solid, heavy stomach and enormous thighs. He walked as if he had consciously to move his legs forward with every step and now, having made the effort to carry

Enys' lunch to him, he lingered by the table looking at the house details Enys had moved aside.

'House hunting are you? Don't envy you, did enough of that a couple of years back and we were only looking at pubs. Seen anything you like?' His voice was thick with a Midlands accent and Enys was inclined to be curt but remembered in time that what he considered to be familiarity was nothing more than the spurious friendship of a professional.

'I've not had much luck so far. I suppose you don't know of anywhere locally, reasonable size, decent garden, usual sort of thing.'

'Funny you should say that, the answer could well just have walked through the door.' The man put a huge hand on Enys' table and turned his bulk clumsily towards a woman who was now sitting at the bar. She was small and poised in a way that made Enys feel threatened, Eloise recalled from the shadows of his mind once more. 'Pammie my darling, come over here a minute, I want to introduce you to –,' he looked towards Enys, raising his eyebrows.

'Enys Williams.' Enys stood up as Pammie Brighton walked towards him carrying her gin and tonic, fox-coloured eyes appraising and approving even before she reached his table. She didn't wait to be asked but sat down and turned to the big man still standing there.

'Jeff, be an angel and bring me a sandwich. You don't mind do you?' She had turned towards Enys as she said this. 'I really do have a house to sell and I'll tell you about it while we eat. I'm Pammie Brighton, by the way.'

Pammie was wearing jodhpurs so tight that they covered her like a pale, corded skin, and a high necked jersey of a good red that emphasised the foxy colour of her hair. She had been riding and her cheeks were still faintly flushed, the colour adding attraction to her unexpectedly plain face. Enys was alarmed: that she was sexually confident he could see and that she meant trouble he was sure. He had no interest in her other than to listen to what she had to say about the house and good manners alone prevented him from excusing himself, gathering up his papers and leaving.

'Don't let the name put you off,' she said, 'it's "Simla". Isn't that a hoot? My father-in-law, my *ex*-father-in-law actually, lived in India for years and when he came back to Cornwall he built a colonial bungalow for himself and the memsahib. It's a long story how I come to be in possession of it but I don't want to live there and I need the money.' While she was talking Pammie was tearing pieces out of a sandwich, the pink slivers of ham caught by her sharp little teeth reinforcing the resemblance to some feral creature. Enys had ordered them both another drink and Jeff had lumbered over to their table, his small eyes hinting at a smirk. 'You'll have to drive,' Pammie said, 'unless you don't mind risking it with me.' Her eyes told Enys that what she said was not the same thing at all as what she meant and he went to pay for their lunch, waiting until Jeff was in the public bar and he could leave his money with the young barmaid.

The rain which had curtailed the afternoon excursion of Dixie Davey and her mother was sliding inland from the west, the sky as hard and bright as metal behind the clouds as Enys and Pammie Brighton left the pub. They drove along diminishing lanes, electricity wires turquoise green against the sky and the far scenery seeming sharp and clear and very near in the silvery light.

Simla was a long, low bungalow overlooking a wooded creek. There was a fretwork canopy over a stoop which ran the length of the frontage and around the two shorter sides of the building. Green blinds were rolled up inside the windows and an indolent peace seemed to enfold the whole house.

The garden sloped gently down in wide terraces to the river where rotting boards were all that were left of a mooring. It was a curious garden as if someone had been only partially successful in hewing it out of a field, palm trees and groves of bamboo giving an illusion of somewhere exotic and Enys could almost imagine that the clouds which were banked up over the river were mountains from which cool breezes blew in the summer and where the snow lay on the summits all year long.

He walked down the shallow steps from the terrace and strolled down to the water, seeing in his mind's eye the small boat he intended to buy moored at the end of his garden. Pammie sat on the wall and watched him, tall and withdrawn and tantalisingly uninterested in her. When Enys joined her again she handed him the key of the front door, holding it in her palm so that he had to touch her hand. 'It's a bit musty but Mrs Thingy – Pearce, comes in to keep it clean and old Mr Pearce sees to the garden.'

'I noticed that the grass had been cut.' He was polite but unresponsive and although she had tried, Pammie had found out nothing about Enys Williams, his replies to her less subtle questions leaving more unsaid than he told her. Now he unlocked the front door and followed Pammie into the hall of Simla: she was watching to see his reaction, gauging the right moment to pursue her chase.

It was a beautiful house, full of light and with golden wood floors. Everywhere was pale, buff and putty, high-lighted by a particularly deep, bright blue as if the river had been condensed and brought into the house. It seemed to be a leitmotif throughout the two main rooms, which opened into each other and which could again be divided by wide sliding doors. The house appeared to be fully furnished and Enys knew the furniture to be good, the rugs he thought valuable, probably Turkish. He wasn't much interested in the kitchen, which seemed large and well equipped and he moved towards the bedrooms down a passage walled on one side by glass panels which gave a view towards the river where he could see the mountain-clouds now glistening and pillowing with the unshed rain.

Three of the bedrooms were perfectly ordinary, comfortable and pretty, but the fourth was L-shaped, extending into a mirrored bathroom which reflected Enys back to himself wherever he looked, and wherever he looked there was Pammie, plain but bright as a butterfly, always too close and always watching him, avidity and mockery in her face, waiting for him to weaken, to falter, when she would circle round him, poised for the kill. He closed the door, amazed by the vulgarity of the bathroom compared with the constraint of the rest of the house.

'That was the mem.'s bathroom. There were those I believe, who considered her not quite the thing and hinted that my father-in-law had picked her up somewhere where he shouldn't have been at all and that he had to marry her to keep her quiet. I never really understood that, what *do* you think they could have meant?' She gave a tiny laugh. 'Actually she was terribly nice to me and made sure I wasn't cast out penniless into the snow when I left her sod of a son.'

Enys wanted to walk away, not to learn anything about Pammie that he didn't need to know. Instead he said, 'That was unusual surely? You were unhappy in your marriage?'

'I wasn't particularly *unhappy* – but I chose my words accurately.' She laughed her tiny laugh again watching Enys, eyes glinting through lowered lids. He felt punished by his embarrassment, for allowing his curiosity to overcome his reserve and walked quickly back to the hallway of the house. The downpour had started and the panels of glass along the passage were patterned by water in streaks and dots like morse code.

'We can't go now, we'll get drowned.' Pammie had joined him by the front door.

'I need to get back I'm afraid. I'll bring the car up and you can get straight in and I'll drive you home Mrs Brighton.'

'Everyone calls me Pammie – Mrs Brighton is the memsahib. And you haven't told me what you think of the house.'

'I'll fetch the car,' and Enys walked out into rain bouncing upwards, soaking his trousers and running off his silver hair. He felt ridiculous, afraid of a predatory, plain woman, unable to stay alone with her because she reminded him too forcibly of Eloise, disliking the way her bold eyes coveted him and longing for someone quiet and understanding who would accept him as he was, not challenge a masculinity not yet recovered from the sickness of the heart that had so wounded him.

Enys brushed against a hydrangea, too tall and straggly and bearing wet, brown flower heads which drenched his shoulders and suddenly a longing to see Binnie swept through him. He stopped as if he needed to breathe and Pammie, watching from the shelter of the canopy, thought he was going to turn around and come back to wait in the house with her, but he went on to where his car stood, raindrops exploding from its roof like fireworks, determined to shed himself of Pammie Brighton and wondering if even so desirable a residence as Simla was worth the price she was asking. He didn't even ask her how much the house would cost.

8

June

Cora Neville lit another cigarette while she waited for the postman. She had walked with Hannah to the main road and seen her on to the minibus which took her to St Joseph's Centre where she would put socks and slumber masks, toothbrushes and combs into grey plastic cases for an airline whose destinations meant nothing at all to her.

Cora was pleased that Hannah seemed to enjoy her job, leaving every weekday morning with an expectation of pleasure that was always fulfilled. On warm weekends when Hannah was at home, they would go to the beach and Cora rejoiced that in the water Hannah was no different from any of the slim, young girls splashing and swimming in the sunshine. It was only when she tried to walk back to where her clothes were piled on an easily recognised bright towel that people stared at her, aware that her likeness to other young women was an illusion. Cora would dry her and help her to dress, asking her questions which Hannah would answer in her small rushed voice.

Hannah's irregular walk made her tire quickly so Cora

would often pack a picnic into an old straw basket and together they would catch a bus, getting off at random and finding somewhere to stay in the fresh air for as long as they could. Hannah's favourite outing was to Ding Dong mine but they could only go there when Ralph took them out in his car, parking as far up the rough track as he could before helping Hannah over the uneven clumps of heather and coarse grass to the top of the rise where the engine house stood, fields and hedges below it rolling away to the sea. Ralph was the only person whom Cora ever allowed to tease Hannah, approving of the care with which he spoke to her, happy when Hannah laughed at a joke she understood.

In the long, dark evenings of winter Cora had taught Hannah to draw and to paint and to make biscuits for their tea. She hadn't succeeded in teaching her to read but Hannah could recognise her name and she loved to sing, always a beat or two behind the music, small sweet sounds substituted for unremembered words.

Cora had taken Hannah to Sunday School at Wilfred Angove's chapel where she thought that she would enjoy the music and Hannah had been happy there for a while, carefully sticking a coloured picture like a large, holy postage stamp into her membership card every week and looking forward to the outing on Feast Day in the summer. Cora had relaxed a little, until the Sunday morning she noticed a reluctance in Hannah to get dressed; she had lingered over her breakfast, splashing milk around and picking tiny pieces off her banana, something she hadn't done since she was a small child. When Cora tried to ask if anything was wrong, Hannah just shook her head without looking at Cora and went to fetch her coat, walking silently the short distance to the chapel. She had gone through the double doors to the meeting room without a backward glance and Cora had walked home, aware that something was certainly wrong.

Wilfred Angove had come to see Cora and had sat in the kitchen looking around at the collections of stones and coloured glass, broken pottery and shells and glowing feathers that Cora and Hannah had found on their walks and which Hannah loved to sort through, sometimes making little piles of different colours or shapes, sometimes placing her treasures in rows like beads in a whimsical necklace.

Wilfred Angove drank his coffee while Cora waited with some curiosity to see if anything other than pastoral concern had brought him to her door. The silence was beginning to lengthen uncomfortably when the Minister said, in a voice loud enough to startle her, 'Hannah is well I trust? After the little,' a pause, 'incident, on Sunday morning I thought that I ought to come and see for myself that all is well. Regrettable, Mrs Neville, regrettable, but perhaps we should have anticipated something of the sort. Not all our little friends are, shall we say, *comfortable*, with someone afflicted like Hannah.' He gave Cora the smile which so deluded the ladies of his congregation but Cora saw only the hard, grey eyes and was unconvinced.

Cora had looked at him, too angry to speak and Wilfred Angove had put down his cup and saucer and wiped the palms of his hands on his shiny black trousers. His finger nails were dirty and Cora imagined his hands to be soft and sweaty and she looked away in disgust. He had continued, 'Has Hannah – ah – mentioned anything about it?' Cora shook her head and he had gone on, 'I think, perhaps, for everyone's sake, you might prefer to take Hannah out of the Sunday School for a while. I'm concerned mainly for her good you understand Mrs Neville, but I think, yes I really do think, that she might actually *prefer* to be with young people of her own kind.'

Wilfred Angove had never known what to make of Cora Neville; he had expected her to question, to argue perhaps, as the mothers of other children in the Sunday School would certainly have done, reluctant to lose their hours of freedom on a Sunday morning. He was relieved when all Cora did was to stand up and say firmly, 'Please go, Mr Angove. Hannah certainly won't be coming to your chapel again so you needn't concern yourself about her any more.' Her face was white with anger as she said, 'And you'll undoubtedly be pleased to know that I'll make quite sure that she stays with people of her own kind in future.' Wilfred Angove seemed to relax at once and with expressions of apology and regret he left Cora, who knew that there wasn't a child in the Sunday School who would harm Hannah.

Cora thought of how she had waited for her at the top of the steps to the front door that Sunday morning and how she had felt a surge of panic as she saw the way Hannah had walked slowly up the road, her card of coloured stickers clutched to her chest. Hannah, used to the company of adults, was unhappy, and Cora knew that she had been wrong to think that she might enjoy being with children but, Cora thought, she had expected her to be safe.

By the time that the minister had called on her, Cora had already decided not to send Hannah to Sunday School again but there had been something in Wilfred Angove's manner that had made her very uneasy and Cora saw clearly in her mind's eye the pattern of bruises on Hannah's arm, which no amount of gentle questioning had explained.

Cora sometimes went to St Joseph's in the afternoon to bring Hannah home. It took a long time, Cora encouraging Hannah to walk because she knew that she needed the exercise, disregarding the glances of strangers as they conversed, Cora asking questions which she would repeat until Hannah answered. Cora was proud of the progress Hannah had made: whatever she had done in the past she felt was justified by the rescue of this tender, vulnerable child who had been her life and her joy. Cora's sometimes startling outspokenness was a shell within which lived someone whose being was so suffused with love that to expose it would be to enable it to be dissolved by pain and pity. Sadie, so observant and intuitive, knew this, aware that even though she knew her friend's character very well, she knew very little of her circumstances, sure also that there was much to discover.

Cora waited for the postman on the day before Hannah's twenty-first birthday as she had waited on all the previous years. On each birthday and at Christmas a package would be delivered, postmarked Edinburgh and containing money, all of it in £50 notes. There was never a letter and this was no inconvenience to Cora, she knew that it was payment from Hannah's father and she was grateful that he was constant and dependable, honouring the arrangement they had made when Hannah was a child and it had no longer been possible to ignore her slowness or to pretend that she would ever be like other children of her age.

Cora had brought Hannah to live by the sea where the climate was mild and where no one knew them. Hannah's father had bought them the house where they still lived and twice a year he sent them money. It wasn't quite enough but Cora was adept at poverty and managed to earn a little by doing any job she could find while Hannah was safe during the day. By working during the summer she managed to save enough to keep them going through the winter when jobs were scarce and they were as happy as anyone who lived in Trewavas Terrace.

As the postman rattled the flap of the letterbox at the front of the house, Sadie Clements tapped on Cora's back door and let herself in, sure of her welcome and waiting while Cora walked back to the kitchen with several envelopes and a brown paper package in her hands.

'Morning Sadie, no work today?'

'I've got the morning off so I thought I'd bring this round for Hannah and scrounge a cup of tea. *And* I've got something to tell you.' She put a small parcel on the table: it was wrapped in shiny paper and tied with several silver bows which glittered as they caught the light. 'I know she likes pink and Jassy told me that this is this year's collector's piece – whatever that means. It's only a Swatch but I thought Hannah might like it, dear little soul.'

Cora turned away to fill the kettle but Sadie saw tears bright in her eyes and felt a tightening in her own throat.

'You're so good to her Sadie, you always treat her the same as all the others and she'll *love* it, you couldn't have chosen anything better.'

'Are those for Hannah?' Sadie nodded towards the letters that Cora had put on the table.

'Most of it looks like the usual rubbish, but a couple are.' The brown package addressed to Cora herself seemed startlingly conspicuous but she decided to ignore it although she could feel Sadie's interest as clearly as if she had spoken. 'You're bursting with something; what were you going to tell me? Is it too early for biscuits?'

'It's never too early for biscuits, you know that.' Sadie sat down and said in a rush, 'What would you say if I told you that Charlo and I have decided to buy Jericho?'

Cora handed an unopened packet of digestives to Sadie and sat down opposite her, lighting another cigarette while she thought about what Sadie had just said.

'I don't know what to say. I'd have thought it was too big for you, it can't be long before your children start leaving home. Won't you rather rattle about in it?'

'Oh, we can't just *live* there, we've got to make money out of it so we thought we'd do B and B and Charlo will keep on the market garden. It's such a *lovely* house Cora and I've always dreamed of living there. Just fancy, me living in the Big House; there'll be plenty of room for us and visitors and I'm going to build up a restaurant. Can't you just imagine little candlelit tables for two in that gorgeous conservatory and perhaps we could have a four poster bed for honeymooners.'

'Don't you think that perhaps they might prefer somewhere a little less public?'

Sadie's soft shoulders shook with laughter. 'Don't be so silly Cora, I mean in one of the bedrooms. And Ralph says he'll stay on in the garden and, oh Cora, you can work there too and not have to do awful jobs all the time. Well, they'd still be awful jobs I suppose but it wouldn't be so bad doing them together, would it?' Sadie looked like a child and Cora could see Jassy behind the soft, plump flesh and shining eyes, Jassy's vivacity not yet transmuted to her mother's perception and kindness, but the resemblance was strong and Cora understood why Charlo loved Sadie and why Jory was determined to separate Jassy from the other young men who pursued her.

'You make it all sound sensible and possible – can you afford it though?'

'Just about. The bank manager has been quite encouraging and if we sell our house and use our savings we can just manage. I can always do odd shifts at the Adelaide and Charlo says he'll stay on at the Tec. until things build up on the B and B side. We'll be all right as Ralph is going to take over most of the market garden work for the time being and he's thinking of buying a share of it and that'll help too. He's so kind, Cora, I can't imagine *why* he isn't married.'

'You don't really think that Gwen Minto would let another woman near her little boy, do you?'

'Oh Cora, you are awful sometimes.' Sadie was dunking

a digestive biscuit which became saturated and broke off to float scummily in her tea. 'Damn.' She tried to flick the pieces out with a spoon. 'Do you really think Gwen wants to keep him at home? She's so nice I can't believe she'd do anything like that.'

'Doesn't mean she's not nice and I suspect it suits them both but yes, I do think that she sees off anyone who gets too close to him. In the subtlest possible way of course, and I don't suppose she knows consciously she's doing it.'

'Cora,' Sadie hesitated but her nature was not one of restraint and she said again, 'Cora, do you like him especially? I know he's good with Hannah and takes you out and I do wonder sometimes if you might, well – you know – get together.'

Cora gave a hoot of laughter and Sadie plunged on. 'You never talk about Hannah's father and I'm not trying to find out anything, *honestly* I'm not, but aren't you ever lonely on your own?'

Cora looked at Sadie and put out her hand to touch the brown paper package of money which lay on the table between them. 'Not really. I like being on my own, always have done and I've got you and Charlo next door and Ralph takes us out sometimes. Gwen's always nice to me, probably because I'm no threat to her and she knows it, and Binnie Seaton's always been very kind to Hannah.' Cora stopped, the mention of Binnie starting a thought in her mind that she wanted to pursue. 'Probably the only person who isn't nice to us is that old harpie at the church, Pearl Angove, but then, she's not nice to anyone even though she's a good Christian woman.'

'But it's not the same as being married, is it?'

Cora smiled at Sadie. 'Being married suits you, anyone can see that but it doesn't suit everyone and I'm happy as I am. Leave a couple of biscuits for Hannah's tea won't you – if you can restrain yourself that is.'

'Oh Cora, I'm sorry.' Sadie looked down at the almost empty red wrapper. 'Aren't I awful? Why didn't you stop me?'

'Well you eat and I smoke and it doesn't do either of us any good. What's Binnie going to do, do you know?'

'She hasn't said anything and I haven't liked to ask her.'

Cora was amused. 'That's not like you Sadie, you must be slipping and you know I depend on you for all the gossip.'

'You know as much as I do *and* you can see who goes in and out from here. Have there been many people to look at the house?'

'A few people I didn't recognise but I've only just seen that Jericho's for sale. You must've put your offer in quickly.'

'We did: as soon as Ralph said it was on the market. We decided that if we didn't at least try, we'd always regret it and Binnie accepted our offer although it's quite a bit less than she'd asked. You don't suppose she'll accept a bigger offer do you? I couldn't bear to lose it now.'

'Gazump you? That's not Binnie's style at all. If she said she'd sell to you, then she'll keep her word, you needn't worry.' Cora thought of the parcels of good clothes so hesitantly offered to her 'for Hannah' which she unpicked and altered for both of them and of the vegetables so often left by her back door. She would have liked to call Binnie Seaton a friend but some reticence in both women prevented their acquaintance from progressing beyond a certain conventional formality.

Sadie had no such hesitation and Cora envied the confidence with which she confronted everything in life, knowing from a child that she was loved, and sure of her worth. Cora wondered if there were secrets in Sadie's life. If there were, she thought, they would be prosaic, not like those she was sure were concealed by Binnie Seaton's reserve or those which caused Cora herself deliberately to keep her distance from any too intimate an association.

The thought that had started so nebulously a little while ago was still in her mind when Sadie left, after standing in the doorway for five minutes still chatting. Cora sat for a while thinking about Binnie and the handsome, upright man she now knew to be Enys Williams and whom she had seen walking slowly past Jericho several times in the last few days. She had watched with interest as he hesitated at the gate and she had seen that each time he had turned and walked away down Trewavas Terrace and become lost to sight as he turned the corner by Tiverton Villa.

It was outside Tiverton Villa that Cora had first seen Enys Williams one day the previous summer, when her attention had been engaged by the intensity with which he had been looking at the house. From her vantage point behind her heavy net curtains Cora had watched him, unknown but somehow familiar to her. She had seen Pearl Angove pass him, hesitate and then turn back to speak to him and she had seen the reluctance with which he accompanied Pearl out of sight around the corner of the house. Cora had allowed him to slide out of her mind and it wasn't until the day of Richard Seaton's funeral that Enys Williams' face had again come into her mind's eye.

Cora pursued her thoughts to an unsatisfactory conclusion and then reached for the brown package and slit it open, counting out the money from Hannah's father. She put the notes into her handbag before fetching her shawl and taking down a basket from behind the kitchen door: she was going to walk into town to buy party food for tomorrow. Gwen Minto's present was the cake, three layers of sponge with bright pink icing and twenty-one candles, artistry forsaken in the accomplishment of Hannah's pleasure.

If Sadie Clements had talked less or if Cora Neville had not spent time in thought, she would have seen Enys Williams make his now routine short walk from Zion House to Jericho but this morning, instead of hesitating at the gate, he pushed it open and walked resolutely up the drive, acknowledging Ralph standing talking to a dark, dirty, middle aged man who was watching Enys with simian interest.

Enys walked around to the back of the house, reluctant to ring the bell now that he had come, to have to stand in the shadow of Binnie's house, to wait for her to open the sun-blistered green door to him like a delivery man or someone come to mend the washing machine. His mouth was dry and he felt depleted, a small boy again in short trousers, full of bread and jam and admonitions to good behaviour. At the far end of the yard was an empty gateway and beyond it he could see the acid green haze of lettuces partitioned by darker stripes of what he thought must be spring onions.

'Binnie not in?' Ralph had finished talking to the man on the path and had walked over to Enys. 'I'm sure she is, but she probably didn't hear the bell. Come in with me; I ought to tell her that I've given Doddy Rowe some odd jobs to do, I don't want her thinking he's slipped in by mistake.' He opened the door and walked ahead of Enys down a stone-flagged passage towards the kitchen. There was a faint reminder of coffee and burnt toast and the sharp, disinfectant smell of ageing bananas. It seemed familiar and personal, the smell of his own flat which he now thought of only as a memory, the landward leaning trees and soft rain of West Cornwall having seeped in to fill the empty spaces of his mind which had been hollow and purposeless for so long.

The sight of Binnie wearing a faded blue smock and standing by a big wooden table with a letter in her hand seemed to Enys to be appropriate. There was no shock of recognition, no disappointment and little surprise. Binnie was as she had always been, someone towards whom Enys felt an emotion no one else in his life had ever aroused. He was constrained by Ralph's presence, wishing he could have met her on his own.

'Look who I found on the doorstep. You remember Enys Williams I expect?'

Binnie put down her letter but she didn't move towards Enys to greet him as she would a returning acquaintance. 'Hello Enys, it's nice to see you. Ralph told me that you were back in Cornwall, looking for a house I believe.' It was as if two weeks had passed since their last meeting: twenty years of separate lives disappeared, unimportant pastimes which they had played in isolation.

Ralph, mistaking the silence for awkwardness, began to tell Binnie about Doddy Rowe. 'I don't trust the man but he can't do much harm in the greenhouse. I can watch him in there and I'll frisk him before he goes home.'

Binnie poured coffee into three mugs and Enys was moved when she passed him his, black and unsweetened as he always drank it. She didn't look at him and Enys thought of the dried hydrangea heads that had splashed rain onto his shirt at Simla and which had awakened in him the resolve to come and see Binnie: tall and pale and resilient in the rain, he understood now why they had brought her into his mind with such longing.

Ralph and Binnie discussed the day's arrangements while Enys watched them, not listening, absorbing without conscious effort the daily small exchanges which formed their mutual dependence. He heard them talking about the sale of Jericho while he stood in the shadows, the better to be able to observe Binnie.

The blue fisherman's smock hung loosely around her, concealing her body in faded sailcloth, but Enys saw that her wrists were narrow and her cheek bones sharp and he knew that she was too thin. The pale gold hair which she still wore in the style of a medieval page was perhaps a little faded, but her topaz eyes were as clear and quiet as he remembered. He had almost forgotten though that she was so tall and an image came into his mind of Binnie swinging along a plane-shaded pavement between him and Richard, nearly as tall as either of them.

He noticed the lines around her eyes as she smiled and saw the way pain and disillusion had strengthened her expression. He observed all this as a painter might, trying to discern the secrets that underlay the features of the girl he had known.

Enys wondered if Binnie would find him much changed. He ate sparingly and walked a good deal and his waist measured only two inches more than it had twenty years ago. He couldn't help but be aware that he was regarded as handsome although the face that was his daily reflection seemed to him to be unremarkable. He knew that his nose was too big and his mouth, which even in repose looked about to smile, reminded him of a duck's bill. The thick, silver hair which had so attracted attention in a young man, was now only slightly less remarkable. It was his eyes though, once so soft a blue, that showed the bewilderment and disenchantment of trust betrayed. They were now like healed wounds and the openness of his expression had gone forever, only the sweetness of his smile revealing for a moment the truth of his nature.

Ralph finished his coffee, putting his empty mug into the sink as he left the kitchen. Binnie looked at Enys. 'I heard that you've been to see Simla. Did you like it?'

Enys smiled. 'The Cornish Underground – I'd forgotten how quickly news travels down here. Yes, I did like it although Helford's not really the area I'm interested in. I was having lunch in the Lamb and Flag and the landlord introduced me to a Mrs Brighton, who owns the house apparently. D'you know her?'

'Oh yes, I know Pammie Brighton. In fact, everyone knows Pammie Brighton, just as everyone knows that she was Richard's most enduring mistress. She was with him when he died you know.' Binnie seemed detached, as if she were speaking of acquaintances she knew hardly at all. Enys looked at her and she pulled out a chair and sat down. 'Do sit down Enys and don't look so shocked. If I hadn't told you someone else soon would have; besides, I'm sure that James must have told you about Richard's little peccadilloes.'

Enys was still holding his mug and he sat down opposite Binnie, the width of the scarred wooden table between them. He ran a thumbnail down a groove in the grain before he said, 'You know that I've kept in touch with James then? That I've stayed with him at Owles Court and that he always kept me up-to-date about you and,' he hesitated, 'and Jory?'

'Of course. Dear James, he's so discreet but clever enough to convey what needs to be said without words.' Binnie put both her hands flat on the table and Enys noticed with surprise that her skin was dry and stained, the nails short and workmanlike. He wanted to put his own clean, warm hand over hers and to walk with her under cherry blossom or by a dark, unseen sea. Instead he said, 'I'm sorry about Richard; sorry that he treated you so badly; sorry that I left you with him. Sorry, oh sorry for a hundred things.' There was silence between them, Binnie looking at her worn hands, Enys looking at his, clasped around a Naples yellow mug which was sponge painted with an improbable cockerel and dark blue fleur de lys.

'It wasn't your fault Enys and you really shouldn't blame yourself. I didn't have to marry Richard, I could have waited for you and I didn't, but I did try my best you know. Richard and I just weren't right for each other: he was a good father though and loved Jory and did his best for him.' She stopped talking and then said, very quietly, 'I don't think I ever truly loved Richard and since his death I feel as if I've been released from a life sentence. Is that a terrible thing to say?'

Enys shook his head, afraid to speak. Binnie went on, 'I've never talked about any of it you know, not to Katha or anyone and now that you're back I feel as if I might start and never stop. Not like me at all.' She gave a small smile at Enys, tears filling her eyes, but before either of them could speak again the kitchen door opened and Jory came in. He was laughing and talking to someone behind him and as he stopped, noticing the tableau at the table, the little golden face of Jassy Clements appeared beside him.

Binnie turned. 'Darling, this is a very old friend of your father's and mine, Enys Williams. Enys, this is my son Jory and Jassy Clements whose parents are buying Jericho from me. Enys used to live near here and he's moving back to Cornwall, Jory.'

'How d'you do, sir?' Jory shook hands with Enys and Jassy smiled at him. 'I think Uncle James has mentioned you. Weren't you at school with him and Dad?'

'Yes I was, and your father and I shared a house in London for a while.'

'Well, I'm very pleased to have met you and I expect I'll be seeing more of you if you're buying a house down here. Do you sail?'

'I do yes, and I'm hoping to buy something small once I'm settled. Perhaps you'll be able to give me some advice, if you're keen that is?'

'Oh rather, and I'd love to talk to you about it now but we've got to go I'm afraid. Meeting some friends, Mum, won't be in for lunch. Goodbye Mr Williams,' and they were gone.

Enys looked at Binnie, who looked back at him and a smile that came from far beyond distress and separation lit both their eyes. 'So that's Jory. He's old-fashioned Binnie, a charmer.'

'He has been my reason for living and now he's off to Dartmouth and is in love with the prettiest girl in the neighbourhood.' She stood up, unwilling to expose any more of herself to this returned stranger who was yet as familiar to her as her own son. 'Perhaps you'll come to dinner soon and get to know him a little?'

Enys knew that he was being dismissed, but gently, and he put down his mug which he was still clutching as if it were a talisman.

As he walked down the drive he could see the man Ralph had referred to as Doddy Rowe standing, half-hidden by a fir tree watching the tall woman whom he recognised as one of the other guests at Zion House. She was hurrying down Trewavas Terrace, a beige macintosh blowing around her legs: a scarf covered most of her blonde hair and she was wearing gloves. Without thinking about it, Enys realised that she was overdressed for a mild, soft day but gave her scarcely a glance, more interested in Doddy Rowe's furtive watchfulness.

Dixie Davey, unaware of being observed by the two men, was on her way to the estate agent's office. Lily, working in a planned and meticulous manner, had cut from the newspaper details of several small houses and her determination had overridden Dixie's reluctance.

'It's a nice day, duck, we could start looking around if you like.' Lily had spoken confidently and Dixie, dressing carefully in layers of clothes to protect herself from exposure to influences over which she had no control, had agreed to collect the particulars of two houses situated on opposite sides of the town. They were both small, two bedrooms and a bathroom upstairs, downstairs the space arranged to suit their present owners.

Trevean had been built as a fisherman's cottage in an alley behind the harbour. Two small rooms had been made into one by the removal of an internal wall and a kitchen had been built on, reducing a little the size of the back yard. There was no garden but the sunny, whitewashed yard was full of colour. There were a few containers made of clay but chimney pots and painted tins, even old tyres, were filled with bulbs in the spring, small flowering shrubs following them later in the year. The front and back doors were painted the turquoise blue of the sea at Porthcurno and the window frames were sunshine yellow. The effect was startling but somehow engaging, a doll's house among the row of grey granite cottages on either side of it.

No. 3 Parc Gew, on the other hand was only six years old, a neat small house on a neat small estate. It had two separate rooms downstairs and a square of grass behind a low wall of sandy coloured artificial stone. Behind the house there was a longer garden backed by trees, on the far side of which was a field, the boundary of two farms.

It was inevitable, perhaps, that Dixie Davey and Lily Beagerie should each prefer the house of which the other had reservations. Lily had confided in Gwen over tea and Congress tarts in the kitchen, 'It's a nice enough little place Mrs M. but right on the edge of town and too tidy for my liking. I can see that Doreen thinks it would be easy to keep clean but I want to be near things here. I enjoy the Bright Hour on Wednesdays and there's the concerts in the gardens and you just have to sit on the prom to watch the world going by and it doesn't cost a thing. And then there's the Luncheon Club, I'm looking forward to that in the winter. Might even go dancing and find myself a sweetheart; that'd put the cat among the pigeons all right.' She gave Gwen a sideways look. 'Do you ever go dancing Mrs Minto? We could go together if you fancy it.'

Gwen was knitting a dusty-pink cardigan in fine wool and now she changed the work around to start on a pearl row. 'I never did like dancing Mrs Beagerie, not even as a young woman, but a nice crowd goes to the dances, I do know that. You'd soon find friends there.' She counted along the row. 'If Mrs Davey doesn't like Trevean, and it does get noisy down there at night being so near The Ship, what about a compromise. Perhaps you could find something newish but in the town so that you could both have what you want.' She smiled at Lily Beagerie, surprised to find that she was glad that the bizarre little woman had decided to stay in Cornwall. Of Dixie Davey she felt less sure, aware that there were things hinted at by Lily Beagerie of which she was unaware. A less agreeable woman would have pressed for details, pleased perhaps with new scandal to enliven the days, but Gwen Minto was well aware of the dangers of gossip and plied her guest with no questions, content to accept whatever Lily told her without probing.

They had finished their tea and sat, as had become their custom, at the kitchen table. Gwen's needles clicked softly and Lily Beagerie turned the pages of her weekly magazine, wondering at the stories of sex changes and implants gone wrong which seemed to have supplanted the reassuring articles she had always enjoyed. She pushed it away. 'Shan't bother with that again, nothing but filth if you ask me.'

Gwen glanced at the lurid headlines. 'I don't bother much with magazines, I don't seem to have the time any more. To tell the truth I suppose everything takes me a bit longer these days.' She looked at Lily with a grimace. 'Not that I'd admit that to Ralph, mind you.' Gwen put down her knitting and said aloud words which surprised her. 'Sometimes I think I'll have to get some help in the house, just for the heavy work.' The two women looked at each other, collaborators, united in the denial of approaching old age. Lily left her suddenly unsuitable magazine on the table and went to find Dixie.

Dixie had just written BARRY SEMMENS on a clean page of her diary, having surprised the estate agent that morning when he was showing the new girl in his office the real meaning of work experience.

It was just the kind of situation that Dixie liked: Barry Semmens was an ambitious young negotiator in a firm of local estate agents and valuers and she knew exactly how he would react to a letter threatening to tell his wife and his employers what he had been negotiating with Tina Chapman that morning. Just a couple of letters, Dixie thought, mustn't be greedy. She only had time to underline the name in red and slip her diary under a cushion before her mother came into the bedroom.

9

July

Katha was irresolute, her usual reaction would have been to fly to Binnie and accept her friend's pragmatic advice as to the wisest course of action to follow in the situation in which she presently found herself. It had always been like that between them, Katha, headstrong and intractable, too capricious to pursue something which bored her and many things did bore her, success coming too easily to someone with her confidence. Katha was, Binnie had sometimes thought, quite good at everything but not very good at anything.

Binnie, too, had always been confident but only in her own spiritual convictions. Over the last few weeks she had been dismayed to feel uncertainty like the incoming tide washing the shores of her mind, doubt advancing like a wave and retreating, pulling pebbles of belief after it in the undertow of forsaken certainties. She acknowledged that it was her refusal to help Katha which had produced this dichotomy, her peace of mind further unbalanced by her feelings for Casey. Binnie had always kept the conscience of the friendship, protective of Katha and able in the early years to dissimulate without being worried by scruples, to keep her out of trouble. Binnie knew that her regard for the truth had increased as Richard's practise of it had waned. She knew, also, that Katha needed her, so she waited until she judged that Casey would be at a sale, and then she drove over to Rosmorran without telephoning first, just as they had always done.

Katha opened the back door and her Clumber spaniel pushed past her to amble into the yard where he lay down in a patch of sunlight, panting from the effort, the miasma of old age surrounding him. 'Poor old sod, time he was put down. Oh Binnie, I'm so glad to see you.' She stood aside so that Binnie could walk into the kitchen. Binnie was surprised to see how clean and tidy it looked and Katha, always aware of how she thought, laughed. 'Hardly recognise it, do you. I fell on Cherry from a great height and told her she was a lazy slut not employed to school horses but to clean my house. Scared her half to death but here's the result.'

Binnie leaned against the Rayburn, unlit now until the first cold nights of autumn. Katha hadn't moved and now she burst into tears. 'Oh Binnie, it isn't Cherry who's a lazy slut, it's me and I don't know what to do. I've *so* wanted to talk to you but I know you'll disapprove and there's no one else I can talk to. I *can't* tell Casey although he'll guess soon enough.'

Binnie was unnerved by Katha's tears, usually reserved for the death of a dog or flowing unchecked when she was in a serious temper. 'For goodness' sake Katha,' she started and then stopped, realising suddenly what was the matter. She looked at her friend, white-faced, still standing by the door, her nose beginning to run. 'You're pregnant aren't you?'

Katha nodded, tears trickling down her pale cheeks. 'Oh Katha, you're so silly.' Binnie put her arms around her and pushed her gently towards the farmhouse chair where Casey usually sat, shaking the cushion to dislodge a cat with strange black and marmalade stripes. She recognised it as the marauder who had stalked the kitchen the last time she had been here. The antagonism was mutual and it hissed at her before settling down again under the table. 'You should have told me. Am I so disapproving that you couldn't? I'm sorry Katha, truly I am, I've no right to judge you and I'll do all I can to help. If you'll let me: if you want me to.' She looked around for tissues and handed the box to Katha who blew her nose, recovering so suddenly from her despondency that Binnie had to suppress an unkind thought.

'I knew you would if I could just make you listen. I'm in pod all right but,' she looked down at her still flat stomach and Binnie thought she was going to start crying again, 'this does sound awful I know, but you see I'm not *absolutely* sure if it's Casey's.'

'Well, if there's any doubt at all that's a starting point.'

'You're not shocked?' Katha thought of something. 'You don't even seem surprised, you didn't guess did you? I thought I'd been awfully careful; not careful enough though, obviously.'

Binnie wanted to tell Katha of her visit to the farm when Casey had been there on his own, to give it flesh and bones by sharing it with someone else but she knew that she could never do that so she shook her head. 'I only realised it just now – you do look awful you know. Are you feeling ghastly?'

'Absolutely, seriously, bloody awful. And I jolly well deserve to, getting pregnant at my age. Can you imagine what the girls will say, and our friends, and just think, I'll probably have grandchildren nearly as old as my own child. Why did I do it?'

'Are you sure that Casey doesn't know?' Binnie nearly

added, 'he was so upset when I saw him'. Katha shook her head and then closed her eyes.

'Shouldn't have done that. Oh God.' She rushed out of the kitchen and Binnie could hear her footsteps heavy on the stairs. When she came down again she had washed her face and combed her hair. 'Better now, sorry about that.'

'I think Katha, that you're going to have to tell Casey, especially if that little performance is going to be repeated. Are you *sure* the baby isn't his?'

'No, I'm not bloody sure, that's the trouble. Oh what have I done? What can I *do* Binnie?'

'I think,' Binnie said again slowly, 'that what I should do is to pretend to yourself so hard that it *is* Casey's child that you believe it enough to convince him.'

Katha looked at Binnie, shocked into silence for perhaps the first time in their long friendship. 'Lie, you mean,' she said at last.

'Lie, lie and keep on lying. What purpose would be served by confessing the truth? You'd hurt him beyond telling; and the girls, how do you think they'd react? Have some sense Katha and just keep quiet. After all, it may be Casey's child and what's to be gained by destroying his peace of mind?' Binnie stopped, afraid she had gone too far. 'You haven't told whoever-it-is?' Katha shook her head. 'Well, that's no problem then. Only your well known inability to keep your mouth shut.'

'I've never heard you talk like this before Binnie,' Katha looked disconcerted. 'You know I'm not good at keeping my mouth shut; I just think something and out it comes.'

'It's your decision Katha; you asked me what I'd do and I've told you. Whether you act on it or not is up to you.' Binnie looked at Katha, something in her eyes that said more than her words. 'Casey's such a good man I think he'll be delighted – especially if you have a son this time. Try concentrating on that and when you've decided what to do, for goodness' sake tell me, won't you? Now, I'm going to make us coffee; I'd suggest a stiffener but you shouldn't "in your condition".' She laughed and plugged a shining kettle into an electric point wiped clean of finger marks and grime. 'You certainly must have scared Cherry, I've never seen your kitchen so, so – pristine.' They were both laughing when the door opened and Casey May walked in, his face lifting as he saw Binnie and saw, too, that Katha looked happier than she had for weeks.

Binnie wanted to leave, to be back in her secure private world where her thoughts were circumscribed, obedient to her will. She didn't want to be with Katha when she told Casey about the baby: she knew that Katha would tell him at once and Binnie wondered about the influence she had always exerted on her friend. She felt a prickle of unease and decided, even as she sensed it, that the time had come to withdraw from Katha the absolution she had always sought for her transgressions, forcing on her the necessity of choice that habit had eroded.

Binnie was still wearing the old tweed jacket of Richard's that she had arrived in so that all she had to do was to walk out of the kitchen. Neither Casey nor Katha seemed disposed to stop her and she forced lightness into her voice. 'Lovely to see you Casey but I've got to fly. I'd almost forgotten that Sadie Clements is coming to go round the house with me so that we can decide what she wants me to leave for her – curtains, carpets, usual thing.' Binnie picked up her bunch of keys from the kitchen table. 'Phone me Katha and we'll arrange dinner. I want to introduce you both to Enys Williams and there won't be many more opportunities for you to come to Jericho.' She looked at her keys, feeling the weight of Jericho's in her hand, wondering if she would miss it at all once it had been handed over to the Clements. 'Goodbye then.'

She walked to her car, now standing in the diminishing

patch of sunshine where the old dog lay. Binnie could see that he had stopped breathing and hesitated, tempted to return to Katha, knowing how she would grieve, but with new resolution she got into her car and drove away from Rosmorran.

Enys was coming to dinner: Binnie thought four too intimate a number and had telephoned James.

'I'd be pleased to come Binnie my dear, but I'm rather seedy and not good company just at the moment. Perhaps I could join you for coffee?' And so it was arranged that Jory should bring Jassy, their obligation being discharged when James arrived after dinner. Binnie's interest in food, never very great, had diminished even further when she had only herself to please, cheese and water biscuits, melon and China tea being her chosen commons. She was an adequate cook but unenthusiastic and without Katha's panache. Binnie remembered Enys' passion for fish and wondered if it would seem obvious if she baked halibut for him, deciding that asparagus seemed less unsubtle. This would be followed by a casserole, not a daube or a pot-au-feu but a plain casserole of chicken and mushrooms. Binnie thought for a long time about a pudding and then decided to make a cream scented with geranium leaves, something which she herself would enjoy: she would serve it with strawberries sliced into marsala. She wasn't sure about wine and chose at random from the stocks in the cellar, two bottles of claret and an old brandy.

Binnie had thought to eat in the kitchen but decided instead to use the dining room for the last time and was astonished to find it looking neglected. It smelled musty and there were twigs and a fall of soot in the fireplace. She was happy to clean it, scouring and sweeping as if ridding herself of ghosts, trying to recapture something of the warmth that had once filled the room, when firelight had flickered over polished furniture and the boughs of holly and ivy brought in from the woods. It was early summer now and Binnie picked armfuls of flowers from the garden. She had always disliked formal flower arrangements, reminding her as they always did of the Ladies' Flower Rota and its attendant squabbles at St Euny's, and now she stood peonies and stocks in a fat stone jar in the fireplace. She was pleased with the effect and accentuated the flamboyance of the display by filling any spaces between the flowers with frothy heads of alchemilla. She made a low posy of pink rosebuds and baby's breath to put on the table, smiling, thinking of Katha as she did so. She wondered about candles, rejecting them as perhaps a little obvious but she polished the spoons and forks, looking in surprise at the tarnish gleaming bronze and blue on the old silver.

For the first time for months Binnie thought about her clothes and looked for the dress with a long, loose jacket that she had bought to wear at a wedding and still rather liked. It was heavy pale silk, not putty nor beige but a soft fawn colour that flattered her. She decided to wear her mother's pearls and wondered if she should have her hair cut but decided instead to twist it into a low chignon. Binnie's face looked very thin without its frame of hair and she wondered if she looked severe.

Katha was restored to her usual ebullience and there was warmth in the kiss Casey planted on Binnie's cheek. She wondered if Enys would kiss her but she knew that he wouldn't. Jory was playing the host, joking with Katha as he gave her mineral water to drink, handing Casey too large a whisky. Binnie saw Enys before he reached the front door and, excusing herself, she went out of the room. She was conscious of her own footsteps as she crossed the hall, staccato on the tiles, muffled on the old patterned rug. Enys brought nothing with him, as if his presence alone was acknowledgement of his status, and Binnie put out her hand to draw him into her house.

'How nice to see you again, Mr Williams.' Jory held out his hand. 'Mum says that you drink pink gin but I'm not too sure how to make it.'

'*Two* drops only of Bitters, very important that. You'll need to cultivate the taste if you're to be a sailor, Jory. When do you leave for Dartmouth?'

'I'm in the New Year intake. I was going in September but I think Mum still needs me here.' Jory spoke quietly to Enys as he handed him his glass as if they were old friends. 'Uncle James is coming along later. He's not awfully well but he wanted to see you, I think.'

'I saw him a few months ago and no, he wasn't well.' Enys swirled his drink around, wondering if Jory realised how ill James was. 'Difficult time for you, losing your father and now your uncle not too well.' He looked at the boy very directly. 'You needn't worry about your mother though, she'll be all right.' They looked at each other, understanding without the need of further explanation linking them as surely as if Enys had spoken aloud the words unsaid between them.

'Excuse me Mr Williams, Aunt Katha's glass is empty.' Jory moved away while Enys talked to Casey May of horses.

Binnie had found fragile old coffee cups at the back of a shelf in the pantry. She had forgotten about them and she had washed them gingerly, taking pleasure in their lightness and unusual pattern. James, with faultless timing, arrived as the little party was moving into the drawing room. Binnie was happy, gratified that her friends liked each other, amused to listen to Katha and Enys remembering childhood meetings and conscious that Casey and Katha had reached an understanding. Jory and

Jassy seemed disinclined to leave and she noticed the care with which they looked after James. Jassy, smiling and enchanting, sat next to his chair on a small, rather moth-eaten footstool while Jory hovered over both of them. James' hands looked transparent as they lay along the arms of his chair, his face faded and tired, but he spoke entertainingly as he had always done, delighted to hear of Katha's child, showing an informed interest in Enys' plans and charming Jassy into surrender. Binnie watched him covertly and was surprised into confusion to find Enys watching her.

When the Mays had left, James drove himself back to Owles Court after asking Binnie to come and see him. 'There's something I want very much to discuss with you; too tired tonight, will you come soon?' She had kissed his thin cheek and said she would. Jassy said that she was going to take Jory away to walk on the beach and the air that came through the open door behind them was nearly as warm as the day had been. The moon was almost full and Binnie imagined the silver trace of light on the water, the wet sand shining in the pale light.

'You look as if you'd like to walk along the beach as well.' Enys was standing by the back door, one hand in his pocket, one holding a little octagonal cup full of cooling coffee. He didn't want to leave but hardly knew how to stay.

Binnie was covering the dish of strawberries with plastic film. 'My days of walking in the moonlight are long gone, it's Jory's turn now.'

Enys didn't turn round but Binnie heard him say, 'When I get my boat you shall come out with me to look at the stars. They're so clear and bright at sea, like nothing you've ever seen: it's a kind of magic.' Binnie looked at his back, darkness beyond it, except for where moonlight bleached the garden into grey.

'Jory's always loved the sea, ever since he was a tiny

boy. I wish he hadn't changed his mind about going away this September, but he feels he should be here with me and I'm perfectly all right on my own you know.'

'He told me. And I told him that I'll look after you.' Enys had turned around as he spoke and he looked at Binnie who felt as grey and colourless as the moonlit garden. 'You're tired and I must go. But I will Binnie, look after you I mean.' The sweet smile he gave her was direct and the gentleness of his expression well remembered. 'Goodnight my dear, a lovely evening.' Enys put down his coffee cup and wondered to himself why he always seemed to have to hold on to something when he was with Binnie. He let himself out of the back door and Binnie continued quietly to arrange the used dishes for washing up the next morning.

As she rinsed the old, silver-rimmed plates and piled them next to a jug full of spoons and forks she thought about James. She had been troubled by his appearance, the few weeks since she had seen him was enough to emphasise the frailty which was slowly trespassing on his body. James had never had Richard's driving energy but he was determined; persistence replacing stamina, strength of purpose a substitute for vigour, and Binnie was grieved to see him so depleted.

Binnie turned off the light, locking the back door but not slipping on the chain as Jory wasn't yet home. She lay for a long time with her book lying unopened on the sheet and went over in her mind the evening's conversations, wondering if she saw too much in Enys' casual words, knowing that she didn't, that she understood him perfectly.

When James telephoned the next morning she said that she would come to tea and they walked in the garden, hot and heavy after a shower in the morning, her feet pleasurably damp in her light shoes. James had asked her where she planned to live and Binnie had looked at him as if she were considering the question for the first time. 'I don't really know. I suppose I thought I'd have time to look around as I didn't expect Jericho to sell so quickly. I thought it might be difficult as it's not big enough for a smallholding and rather too big for a house in the position it's in. I always imagined that if someone wanted a house with a few acres they'd move out of the town as there's not really a living in a market garden any more, and as I was quite sure that I wouldn't sell it to a developer I thought I might be there for some time. It seems though that it's just what the Clements want and I must say that it seems a good idea to turn it into a small hotel or whatever.'

'You won't mind?'

'Heavens no, not a bit. But I suppose I *should* find somewhere to go.'

The air was again full of light rain and they had walked back to the house before James said, 'Binnie, I don't know if you'll think this a bad idea but would you consider living here?' He spoke hesitantly. 'I don't need a companion so please don't think that's behind my question. It's just that I thought that if you liked the idea at all, you could live at Owles Court until Jory wants to use it and then there's always the Lodge or one of the farmhouses.' He looked at her; the room was growing dark too early and he put out a thin hand to switch on a lamp. 'I always thought I'd pass it straight over to Jory but I've rather given up on that idea.' There was a cyclamen in a blue and white pot on the table beside the lamp and as Binnie tried to think of what to say, two bruised red petals fell on to the dark wood and she imagined that she heard them fall.

'Will you let me think about it James? It's something I hadn't considered and I'll need to talk to Jory of course.' She added after a pause, 'It might suit us all very well though.'

'I wondered, you see, whether you would take over the garden if that's what you'd enjoy. Selfish of me I know but you have such a feel for plants, Binnie, that it seems a pity not to use your skill. Perhaps I shouldn't say that, it might be construed as undue pressure wouldn't you say?' James laughed. 'Tea, I think. Will you try my new green tea from China? It was delivered this morning and I made myself wait until you came before I could taste it.'

They went on to talk comfortably as old friends do of other old friends. 'Did you hear that Enys has been to see Simla? I went once or twice when the old Brightons lived there and remember it as a very comfortable house but not, I think, right for Enys.

'Next time he's over here I thought I might ask him to have a look at some of the stuff around the place. There's far too much of it and Enys knows quite a bit about antiques, but I'm sure that you know that.'

They talked of Jory and of Jassy and of the Clements' plans for Jericho. James asked after Katha and Binnie told him that Doddy Rowe was out of prison and doing some casual work in the market garden. She told him, too, of seeing Pammie Brighton as they had eased past each other in a traffic jam on the Truro road. 'Awful, James, not knowing where to look although Pammie seemed quite unabashed to be seen with someone else's husband.'

'I suppose,' he said, 'that she's had a certain amount of practice, and I did hear that Lizzie Olver's left Brooke because of Pammie and that Brooke intends to marry her.'

'Where on earth do you hear things like that James, I never do. Poor Lizzie.'

'This time, my dear, I think perhaps you should save your sympathy for Mrs Brighton.' Binnie was startled and James went on, 'Never known anyone as rough on his horses as Brooke Olver.' He looked at her. 'She'll need everyone's pity before she's done with a man like that.' Binnie looked unconvinced and James changed the subject. 'Now, let me tell you about my plans; in a few weeks I thought I might go with a friend to Salzburg – I feel a need to see it again. Have you ever imagined what it would be like to have been born deaf and never to have heard Mozart, can you imagine the loss?' He looked at her with a smile, not expecting an answer.

They drank green tea and took pleasure in each other's company and Binnie began to think that it might be just what she needed, to live in this safe, sturdy house for a while with someone who made no demands on her and whose company she so enjoyed. She drove home through the drizzle of the summer evening to the place where she had lived ever since her marriage and she knew that she was right to leave it, knowing too that James had not spoken carelessly of Enys and she wondered what he had been trying to tell her.

Binnie needed to think about moving to Owles Court, to imagine herself waking up in the morning to an aspect other than the one she had known for twenty years, to the sun slanting in a different direction from the one she was used to, to the sound of rain on leaves not familiar to her. She knew the house well, knew the park and the stables as if they were her own garden but she wondered how she would feel, aware that someone else was living under the same roof but separated from her by election.

James had suggested that the rooms on the east side of the house would easily convert into separate quarters for her. She would have a staircase of her own and her own front door. Work could start as soon as she had made up her mind, to enlarge the butler's pantry into an adequate kitchen and a bathroom could be made from one of the bedrooms on the floor above. He had also made it clear that her privacy would not be broached and that they would operate entirely as individuals, meeting when it was expedient, perhaps a little oftener than they did at present.

It was the garden, as James had known it would be, that weighted Binnie's decision. Owles Court had a rhododendron walk that filled the spring with colour, the air with the sweetness of honey. Camellias grew there, glossy-leaved and tender-flowered, and the woods were as full of bluebells as the hedges were of primroses. It was the formal gardens though that James had offered as bait and Binnie, with only a slight hesitation, rose out of the water and happily and knowingly took it. There was no doubt that the gardens were becoming neglected, the students who came to work for a month or two were no substitute for the men James' father had employed. Ted Rogers had worked at Owles Court for twenty-five years and he missed James' steady precision at his side. There was, he thought, a limit to what he could achieve on his own.

From the time she had moved to her uncle's vicarage Binnie had never lived in a small house and she realised quite suddenly that she was looking forward to moving to Owles Court where she would have all the space she was accustomed to, and she was grateful that the question of where to live need no longer occupy any of her thoughts. She was happy to let the Clements have all the time they needed to sell their house and she set about preparing to leave Jericho.

Jory helped her as much as he could but there was something she felt that she needed to do on her own and one morning of threatening clouds she once again climbed the stairs to the attics. From the vicarage trunk she took out the parcels of baby clothes that had caused her such anguish when she had first discovered them and she took them down to the kitchen.

The weather was curious: ever since the spring it had rained in what felt like unceasing streams and as summer had overtaken the spring the rain had continued. There were hot days of course when mist rose from the sodden land, and when the sun shone it brought crowds of thankful holidaymakers to the beach intent on salvaging something of their fortnight. When Binnie walked along the promenade on the damp, grey days of that summer, she saw that there were always one or two small groups on the beach. Mothers, strangely always mothers, huddled in plastic macs or thin cagoules, watching while children dug in the gritty sand, damp hair sticking to their faces, teeth chattering with cold. Mostly people walked around the town, eating their hamburgers or fish and chips in whatever shelter they could find. Binnie was always conscious of her good fortune in living in the warm, comfortable house that people looked at covetously as they passed by, but she alone was aware of how much she envied those mothers with cold, mottled legs who sat and watched over their children on the windswept beaches.

As Binnie unfolded the tissue paper that covered each little piece of baby's clothing she smoothed it flat and folded it into a neat oblong. When she had unwrapped everything that she had brought from the attic she realised what she was doing and took all the old yellow paper out to the dustbin. It was drizzling again but the air was warm and she could smell the sharpness of wet nettles in the rain and she stood enjoying it before going in to wash the baby clothes. She looked them over carefully; there were no moth holes and they were not discoloured so she put aside the pilches, smiling at the anachronism of the idea, and made a lather of soap flakes in the sink.

The little woollens were so fine that they felt like silk as they slipped through her hands and she rinsed them gently, rolling them in a towel before laying them out flat to dry on the floor of the dining room. She could think of no better use for them than to give them to Katha, wishing with all her heart that she could use them herself. She knew that Katha would toss them into the washing machine and she hesitated at the thought of those fine, tiny clothes shrunken and felted but she wanted Katha's baby to have something lovely at least once. Casey's baby too, for Binnie was sure that Katha was carrying her husband's child and she dried her hands thinking of Casey's brown arms holding the baby who would be born at the end of the year and remembering being held herself so safely in their comforting circle.

Binnie made herself a sandwich and went to eat it standing by the back door so that she could listen to the rain, for Binnie loved the rain. She loved the way it enclosed her in a private world where the treachery of an intermittent sun was excluded and where there was nothing unpredictable to contend with. Binnie was happiest when it rained, she had no need to find excuses to stay at home and she gardened through all but the heaviest downpours dressed in Richard's old waterproofs and boots.

When Enys turned the corner by the big glasshouse, he stopped to look at Binnie. She had a thick sandwich in her hand and an expression of such wistfulness on her face that he was taken aback and wondered if he should turn around and leave before she saw him. He was too late; Binnie raised a hand, her face falling instantly into its usual self-containment but not before Enys had seen what he had hoped for, an openness to feeling that he had feared was lost forever from Binnie's face.

'I see you still enjoy the rain.' He walked slowly towards the back door, raindrops like silver beads on the suede shoulders of his jersey. 'I often thought of you when it rained. Do you remember when we walked down Farm Street and you were wearing a white dress with some sort of shiny bits on the skirt and how it rained and rained?'

'We were both soaked through and we went into the church and . . .'

'. . . And I kissed you. Kissed you in the porch of the Catholic church, half expecting a thunderbolt to come crashing down on us.' Enys was standing very close to her and he could see the memory very clearly in her eyes. 'That was the night . . .'

'Have you eaten?' Binnie interrupted him, the moment deliberately broken. She went on, 'Bread and cheese on the kitchen table if you fancy it. Actually I'm glad you've come, there are some things I want to get rid of and James said you know about antiques. I could do with some advice.'

'Quotations given free. No obligation.'

Binnie laughed and closed the door. 'James has suggested that I might go and live at Owles Court. Not with him, of course, but in the east wing and I *think* I've decided to go.' She looked at Enys who was cutting thin slices of cheese. His face was expressionless and Binnie wondered if he'd heard what she'd said. 'I said that I might go to live at Owles Court.'

'I heard you. I was thinking about it.' Enys stopped buttering the bread. 'Binnie I think I should tell you that James has asked me if I would like to live at Court Farm. As a matter of fact he thought I could start a business there, selling antiques, and like you I'm almost sure that I'll accept.'

'What about Simla?'

'I couldn't live there. You'd hate it, wouldn't you?'

'Oh Enys, I'm sorry. You liked it so much.'

'It came with too many appurtenances, is that the right word? What I mean is that Mrs Brighton seemed to be part of the deal and I just wasn't interested.' Enys had made two sandwiches as he spoke and Binnie poured coffee into mugs, passing him one and taking hers to her usual chair by the Rayburn.

'Court Farm's quite the nicest house, do you know it?' Enys shook his head. 'What about James' idea of an antiques business, would you like that?'

Enys finished eating, then he said, 'James is extraordinary isn't he? He seemed to pull all my vague ideas together and come up with a plan that feels as if I'd thought of it myself and is just what I *would* have thought of if I'd been a bit cleverer.'

'He's asked me to take over the gardens.' They smiled at one other. 'I'd never have thought of *that* but it seems more and more that it's just what I want to do.' She said in a rush, 'I shall miss him so much.'

There was no need for her to explain what she meant and Enys said, 'He's not dying yet Binnie. He could live for a long time you know. I think he's just putting his house in order and we're part of it.'

'Do you want to sell antiques Enys? I didn't know you were serious about it; I didn't even know you knew much about antiques until James told me. In fact,' Binnie said, 'I don't know much about you at all any more, do I?'

'Have I changed so much?'

Binnie shook her head. 'You've changed hardly at all, and except that we're both older, I feel as if you've scarcely been away. What I meant was that I don't know what's happened in your life, why you look so sad sometimes and why you never touch me any more, not even my hand.' She gave a little smile, 'And I don't know what I'd do if you did.'

Had it been anyone else sitting in her kitchen on this unseasonal summer's day, Binnie would have cleared away the debris of the meal and washed the plates, putting the drying up cloth to air on the rail of the Rayburn. With Enys, all she wanted was for him to tell her why he had divorced his wife, what she had done to him to make his once familiar face look overwhelmed with loss. She wanted to know if he had loved her, the woman who had hurt him, as he had loved Binnie herself under the plane trees, in a white cotton dress from which the rain ran in coloured streamers from the spangles on her skirt.

It had rained that summer too, just as it was raining now, when she and Enys and Richard had been young and inseparable and it didn't seem to matter whom she loved. It mattered now though and looking at Enys, Binnie realised that he wasn't the boy of twenty years ago who had gone to Berlin leaving her with his best friend and whose wishes for their happiness seemed the only necessary blessing on their marriage.

Enys was talking again. 'Do you remember my step-father?'

'Hardly, but I've heard of him from Richard and James.'

'When I left Eloise I was,' Enys stopped for a minute, and then went on, 'not very well really. A bit off balance for a while and the only place I could think of to go was to my mother's and stepfather's house. My mother was bound up in her own interests and I was, as I'd always been, a bit of a nuisance to her, but my stepfather looked after me and when I was a bit more human again he started taking me to auctions. Funny how you can live with someone for half your life and not know things about them isn't it?' Binnie sat watching him. 'He'd been going to auctions for years apparently but I'd never known and my mother wasn't interested. Anyway, he started taking me and I learned a good bit, watching and listening. I liked glass especially, something about the thought of generations of people using it, careful hands preserving it and its fragility enduring. Am I making sense?'

'Perfect sense.'

'We used to have to use guile about keeping our treasure

as my mother didn't like the house to be untidy and when the dear old boy snuffed it, I found a box or two of unsorted glass in the cellar.' Enys stopped and looked at Binnie. 'If you don't know about glass this won't make much sense to you, but to me it was like finding the treasures of Montezeuma.

'There was a box of wine glasses, good ones by Beilby, and I knew they were worth a few hundred each so I put them to one side and then, at the bottom of the box wrapped in tissue paper, was an enamelled Armorial glass.' Enys looked at Binnie to see if she understood. 'It had an opaque twisted stem and when I sold it,' he took a deep breath, 'it made enough, with my savings, for me to be able to buy a house.'

'Oh! Enys. Did your stepfather know, do you suppose?'

'I like to think that he did and that he left it like that for me to have the pleasure of discovering it.' Enys looked as if he were listening to someone unseen, then, turning to Binnie, 'Yes, I think he must have done. He knew enough about glass to realise what he had – it's the kind of discovery that a small collector like he was dreams of and I felt – feel – that he was telling me what to do: that he knew what direction I should take to make a new life for myself. Does that answer your question?'

'I'm glad the direction was back to Cornwall.' Binnie looked at him and saw a man she had known in her heart all her life and loved as she had loved no-one else. The affection she felt for Ralph, the way she loved James and the guilt of her feelings for Casey were swamped by the tidal wave of knowledge that Enys was part of her, that years of marriage and bringing up Jory had never changed the feeling of belonging that had started the day he held out his hand in that long-ago London garden and said, 'Enys Williams,' and smiled at her with his denim blue eyes.

Enys was watching her. 'Where else should I have gone? If Richard had been alive it would have been different. I'd never have come back, although I had thought that perhaps I might but I couldn't have seen you unhappy with him, it was hard enough just to know that you were. No,' he half smiled at her, anticipating her question, 'James didn't tell me but I could sense it. I think if things had been all right we should have been able to be friends but James knew the danger and never suggested we meet.'

It was very quiet, rain sliding silently down the big window over the sink. 'Where's Jory?' Enys broke the silence. Binnie put her mug down and locked her fingers together, stretching them as if they were stiff like an old woman's.

'Out with Jassy I expect. Weren't they sweet with James the other night? They didn't have to stay you know but I was so pleased that they did.'

'Does Jory know, Binnie?' Enys asked the question quietly and Binnie shook her head.

'I've never had any reason to tell him, couldn't really. Would *you* have told him?'

Enys looked at her for a long time before finally saying, 'No. No, I couldn't have told him either although,' he stopped and looked at her again, 'I'm almost sure that he *does* know. Nothing he's said, just a feeling.'

Enys stood up and walked over to the farmhouse chair where Binnie was sitting. He put a hand on each arm of the chair and kissed her upturned face very gently.

'Just call it a father's intuition,' he said.

10

September

When Gwen Minto admitted to Lily Beagerie that she felt the need of help in the house, it was as if the disparate elements of a complicated design had suddenly arranged themselves as a completed picture in Lily's mind. She had been turning over the difficulty of resolving the problem of where she and Dixie would live once she had sold her London home, determined now not to exile herself to the neat modern house that Dixie favoured. Lily needed to consider carefully how to present her plan to Dixie but years of unobtrusive watchfulness had given Lily the ascendancy in their relationship and she foresaw no difficulty which she couldn't overcome.

'You'd better come to London with me duck, things of yours I expect you'd like to sort through on your own. Going to put it all in store and we can send for it when we move in down here.' Lily was eating pale, soft squares of clotted cream fudge. Having worked her way through the ten flavours on offer she had settled on mocha as her favourite and she bought a quarter every other day, walking along the promenade in all weathers to the sweetshop on the corner where several small cafés and gift shops broke the line of grey terraced houses and private hotels.

'Have a bit of fudge?' She held out the bag to Dixie.

'No! For goodness' sake Mother you'll rot your teeth with that stuff.'

'Better take 'em out then.' Lily made a movement towards her mouth, diverting her hand towards the paper bag on her lap. 'I've been to see the Clements,' she said indistinctly. 'Made an offer for No.3. A good offer and they're thinking about it.' The fact that Sadie and Charlo had readily accepted Lily Beagerie's offer and that contracts were already being drawn up was something she thought better concealed for the time being. 'Sure you don't want some fudge?'

'For God's *sake* Mother. I don't *want* the fudge and I don't *want* to live at 3, Trewavas Terrace. Whatever made you think I would?'

Lily wiped her fingers on her handkerchief and without looking at her daughter she said, 'I made up my mind that I wanted to stay near the friends I've made and I like that house. I can afford it and if you want to live with me you'll be welcome and if you don't, well, you can lump it.'

'I've no say in the matter at all?'

'Not this time duck. You don't have to live with me if you don't want to: I've got my pension and I thought I might take in a couple of lodgers to help with the expenses and I'm going to see if young Carol wants to come back with us.'

'Carol! You do mean *cousin* Carol? Mother, she's a punk, she calls herself Caz or something and she's got a stud in her nose. You *can't* have her to live with us, she'd never fit in.'

'Live with "us", is it? You've decided to stay with me then? Didn't take you long to make up your mind and

Carol isn't the only one who's changed her name is she?' Lily's triumph was only partially hidden by the dark glasses which no amount of cajoling or mockery from Dixie had persuaded her to abandon. 'Anyway, I like Carol or Caz or whatever. She's had a hard time trying to get a job; been on all those daft schemes and nothing's been permanent but I've got a job in mind for her. Don't ask me what it is because I shan't tell you.'

'I wasn't going to ask.' Dixie's mouth was tight with annoyance. 'I suppose I'd better come with you, but you might have given me some warning, it'll mean rearranging all my projects.'

'That's a good girl; anyway, it'd be a waste of a ticket if you'd decided not to.'

'You've already bought them?'

Lily snapped open her handbag and showed Dixie the two coach tickets she had bought that morning. 'I know you, you see my duck, and I know this is best for both of us. I want it to be a fresh start and we'll give young Carol a helping hand as well. What d'you say?'

Dixie Davey looked at the old woman in the raffish yellow and black checked skirt, at the pink hair and the sleeveless blouse and something she scarcely recognised any longer as love tried to find expression in her voice. She stretched out a big, ugly hand. 'Give us a bit of fudge then, you old bat.' To Lily Beagerie it was enough.

Lily's London house was not unlike No. 3, Trewavas Terrace but instead of Cornish granite shining with flecks of mica, it was built of yellow brick, pitted and spalled by attack from smoke and the polluted air. It was on a main road and the noise of buses passing every few minutes and the unending flow of cars had been somewhat lessened by double glazing. The winking of neon lights across the front of a drinking club on the other side of the road and the nocturnal glare of sodium street lights however, was something that even drawn curtains seemed unable to subdue. Lily, who was accustomed to living in London, thought nothing of these disadvantages, in fact she had always rather liked the vibrancy and immediateness of the noisy evenings and the vicarious life of the streets. She saw little of her large, dispersed family and Dixie discouraged friendship with neighbours, drifting and impermanent as they were, one young couple replacing another, black and white, never settling for long in the bedsits or small flats into which most of the houses on either side of Lily's had been converted.

Lily's house stood out from the others, painted every two years and well maintained. She had long ago given up her struggle with the garden and it was now paved with green slabs, a few shrubs still insistently alive, decorated like outlandish Christmas trees with crisp packets and cigarette cartons, empty drinks cans and, to Dixie's further indignation, occasionally a condom, thrown over the wall with casual disregard for the proprieties.

Lily and Dixie had left the London-bound coach by the Town Hall, opposite the soot blackened tower of St Alphage's. The house was marooned on a mournful little promontory, traffic like twin rivers in spate rushing past on either side of the houses and the railings of a small park which was the Council's token nod towards conserving the environment.

It had rained most of the way up from Cornwall and Dixie felt sticky and uncomfortable and slightly sick from the cheese and tomato sandwiches she and her mother had eaten at midday. She wanted a bath and the security of her own bedroom. Lily seemed unaffected by the humidity and walked briskly across the road, dodging motorbikes and cars with remembered skill.

The bushes in the green concrete garden had flourished

in the unaccustomed summer rain and needed to be cut back and tidied but Lily was pleased to see the house looking trim and homely. She made a mental note to wash the paintwork and clean the windows but she was sure there'd be no difficulty in selling it and tomorrow she would put that in hand. Now, what she needed to do was to settle Dixie and then she would ring her sister Ellen and ask about Carol.

Lily was not really worried about Dixie although she was very cheerful, too cheerful, and Lily had learned to distrust these occasions of exhilaration as the forerunner of a period of intense activity on Dixie's part when she would lock herself in her bedroom, later slipping out of the front door when she thought that Lily's attention had slackened, to hurry to the post box on the corner, her hands filled with letters. The conspiracy between mother and daughter about Dixie's true mission in life had persisted for so long that Lily knew that she was caught in a lie which suffocated her and allowed her to live her life in only one dimension. Her nature was candid and she was aware that the secrecy which had become second nature diminished her and she was determined to put an end to Dixie's blackmail and to start a life of openness and uncomplicated truthfulness when they moved into their new home in Cornwall. In Gwen Minto she had found a friend whose integrity was everything Lily Beagerie would have chosen for herself and she was happily surprised to find that someone so transparently good could be both joyous and even bawdy on occasions.

Dixie had put the kettle on for tea and was carrying her mother's bright brown plastic travelling bag upstairs when the telephone rang. It was Ellen, and Dixie, lingering on the stairs, heard her mother arranging to go out to lunch the following day. 'I'll get the eleven o'clock bus when I've been to the estate agent, be with you in time for a good old

chat. Carol'll be there won't she? Oh Caz, nearly forgot.'
Lily laughed. 'Tea time? That'll do. Not got a job has she?
That's good. I've got lots to tell you duckie, have the kettle
on. Ta then.'

Dixie put the bag on Lily's bed and went into her own
bedroom. She opened the window for some air, closing it
again quickly against the noise and smell of diesel fumes.
If her mother were to be out all day it would give her
time to sort through her notebooks and files and to burn
anything that it would be unwise to keep.

'If you don't mind Mother, I won't come to Aunt
Ellen's tomorrow. I thought I'd make a start on sorting
my things and I must say the sooner we can leave here
the better. Now I'm used to the idea I'm looking forward to
moving, although I'm still not sure about living in Trewavas
Terrace.'

'You mean you're not sure about being so close to other
people, don't you? Listen my duck, I won't always be
around to help you and I want to see you settled down
Doreen. I want you to make a proper break, give up the
letter writing and start with a clean slate in Cornwall.
Nobody knows us there, nobody knows anything about
us and we can think of something for you to do. And
besides, we'll have young Carol with us and she's sharp
as a needle, wouldn't do for her to suspect anything would
it now?'

Dixie's face was expressionless. 'I've got a lot of out-of-
date papers I don't want to take with me so I thought
I'd burn them. Is there anything I could use for an
incinerator?'

'Probably an old oil drum in the shed.' Lily looked
at her daughter as if she were going to say something
more but had changed her mind. 'How about fetching
in fish and chips tonight? We could do with something
hot. Sodding rain's followed us up here: seems wetter in

London somehow and the house smells a bit musty. I'll get a nice floral spray tomorrow and squirt it round a bit.'

'I could ring the storage people if you like.' Lily was pleased. 'And Mother,' Dixie said slowly, 'I think you're right to help Carol. I only wish someone had tried to help me.' Dixie's voice was quiet, normal in a way that Lily hadn't heard for a long time.

'I know, my duck, I know. But it's all going to be better from now on, trust your old mum.'

Ellen Byrne was twenty years younger than her sister, the alpha and omega of a family of eight. Her home in an outer suburb was in the middle of a long, straight road of respectable red houses. Timid Dutch gables enlivened each frontage and red and black lozenge-shaped tiles made a pathway from the pavement, through a sheltered porch where it paused to overcome two steps, then pursued its course to the front door. Each house was separated from its neighbour by a privet hedge except where the original walls of glazed dark brown brick stood as they had done since the road was built. Nearly all the houses had white-painted woodwork, the impression they gave to a casual observer was that they had survived exactly as their Edwardian builder had intended. No one had replaced the sash windows with white plastic frames nor covered the red bricks with rustic stone; no carriage lamps, no roof extensions, no glass-panelled front doors. It was, thought Lily Beagerie, a picture of upright, complacent suburbia and as dull as ditchwater.

She had never understood how Ellen could live in a street where the view from the windows was a mirror image of her own tidy, unchanging house: no shops near enough to which she could pop out without her coat, no markets nearer than a bus ride away; no life, no colour, only carefully preserved cars and tidy front porches and long, quiet back gardens where you visited by invitation. It wouldn't have suited Lily but Ellen liked it. She had lived there for nearly twenty-five years, ever since she and Eddie Byrne had moved into two rooms of his parents' house. Carol had been born there two years later and when Eddie's father had died, they had colonised the main house, taking possession of it entirely when old Mrs Byrne had followed her husband to become a rose bush in the crematorium garden.

As Ellen had aged she had become more like Lily and to see them together was to suppose them to be mother and daughter. The resemblance was superficial however and behind the two new-moon-shaped faces very different characters were revealed. Lily's face was wary, amused and faintly malicious, her feelings partly camouflaged by the dark glasses which had become a permanent feature of her armoury. There was stoicism in the set of her mouth and her candyfloss hair seemed like a flag of convenience under which sailed a well founded and diverting vessel.

Ellen's face was softer, more gullible, less mischievous than her sister's. Twenty-five years of living with small, noisy Eddie Byrne and his large and boisterous Irish family had settled contentment on her features for they had been very happy together, their wedding picture capturing her forever in long, white patent leather boots and a crocheted dress which had left her shivering on the steps of St Francis Xavier's, where flurries of snow had swirled around them like colourless confetti.

Lily had always been thin but Ellen, a plump young woman, had become fat in middle age. Eddie saw no difference in her and they had both expanded gently and in accord, seeing the friends they had grown up with, taking holidays each year in the same two or three resorts which they knew they would enjoy and shopping together at the supermarket every Thursday evening. Eddie cut the grass and papered the walls and Ellen knitted cardigans; he brought her tea in bed every morning and she cooked him steak and kidney pudding once a week.

·Carol had been brought up in this dull and loving home, a girl who was almost beautiful and certainly cleverer than both her parents put together. For most of that time if there had been any discontent on her part it had been concealed, but then, during the summer when she turned sixteen, Carol changed 'almost overnight' according to Ellen. Black dye stained the turquoise tumble twist in the bathroom, incense flooded through her bedroom door and her neat, careful clothes were swapped for the torn and threadbare outfits like those of the young men and women who shuffled inarticulately through Ellen's polished and hoovered house. Eddie had laughed and said she'd grow out of it. 'Just a phase she's going through, she's still our lovely girl underneath all that muck.' Ellen had tried to take an interest in the nose stud, worrying about what would happen when her daughter had a cold, but when Carol came home with the hair behind her ears shaved off leaving only a tuft at the back of her head, she found that interest waned, and was replaced by vexation. The only thing that hadn't changed about Carol was her intelligence but every job she applied for was 'regretfully filled' when she went for an interview and the youth training schemes she undertook to prepare her for work left her cynical and determined not to compromise.

Lily got off the bus and turned towards Ellen's house. She was carrying two custard slices in a gold cardboard box and she scrambled to step down to the pavement before the driver slammed the door on her. At least it wasn't raining, she thought as she paused by the wrought iron gate to transfer the box to her other hand. Ellen had seen her struggling and opened the front door, waddling down the path to meet her.

'No Doreen with you? I've got a lovely pie for lunch, shame she hasn't come. Come on in Lily, you're looking really well, must suit you wherever you've been staying this time. Somewhere in Cornwall isn't it?' She took the cake box and carried it through to the kitchen. 'Carol says she'll be sure to be here at tea time and she's looking forward to seeing you.' Ellen stopped suddenly and looked at her older sister. 'My God Lil, you should see her, tattoos on her arms and black boots a navvy'd wear. No wonder no one'll give her a job.'

'Don't you worry about that any more duckie, I've got a job for her and as for all that silly stuff, well, you don't want to take any notice of that. Do her the world of good to get away for a bit, see how the other half lives – and a bit of sunshine and sea air never did anyone any harm. Now, where's those cream slices. I'll put them out while you make the tea.'

The sisters spent a happy day together: at midday they took their pork pie and salad outside to eat in the cool of the garden, sitting at the wooden table Eddie Byrne had made for Ellen. Lily told Ellen about the house in Trewavas Terrace and her new friends, Gwen Minto and the Clements and Pearl Angove who wasn't as bad as everyone made out. Ellen's stories were of the Byrnes: of Eddie's Aunt Terry who took to her bed when she was jilted at the altar and stayed there, communicating with her family through St Agnes, virgin and martyr, for thirty years until she died; of his cousin, Lucky Joe Byrne, who thought he'd won the Irish Sweepstake but couldn't find his ticket and never got over it. Lily had heard these stories before but she enjoyed watching Ellen's face as she told them, her cheeks and chins joggling as she laughed.

'Tell me about Carol,' Lily said and Ellen wiped her hot,

perspiring face and turned to look at the sister who had been like a second mother to her.

'You'll see for yourself Lil; she's just the same as before you went away. I don't much mind *what* she looks like but I wish I thought that she was happy.' Ellen concentrated for a minute. 'I don't think she's *that* unhappy mind you, but a clever girl like my Carol could do so much if someone'd give her a chance.' There was no need for her to say what they both understood, that Carol, with her lovely face hidden under thick, white makeup and her clean but depressing clothes, had no chance at all of being chosen by an employer unless she conformed to a pattern which she seemed determined to resist.

Ellen fetched two cans of ginger beer from the fridge and handed one to Lily. 'Ta duck, nicest drink of all in the summer,' Lily said. They sat for a while watching the fountain that Eddie had installed splashing and trickling over cunningly contrived waterfalls. 'Must be my age but it makes me want to pee, that does,' and Lily tottered up the path in her high heeled white sandals, the tender parts of her toes cushioned by pink elastoplast.

'That's better.' She sat down again and poured the rest of her ginger beer into a glass decorated with oranges and lemons. 'Before Carol gets here I want to tell you what I'm going to suggest to her, don't want you to get the wrong idea or anything. You remember I told you about my friend Gwen Minto where I've been staying? Just the other day Gwen was saying that she needs some help in the house. Well! What could be better? Carol could work for her and live with me and Doreen just round the corner. What d'you think of that?' Before Ellen could say anything Lily Beagerie went on, 'If I'm honest duck, I wasn't just thinking of Carol, but with someone else in the house Doreen would have to be a bit careful – you know what I mean.'

'No better then?'

Lily shook her head. 'Perhaps a bit, I don't really know. All I do know is that she's burning stuff today; that must be a good sign, and she says she wants Carol to have the chance of changing her life; the chance that I was never able to give her.' Lily stopped and Ellen saw suddenly that she was old.

'It isn't your fault Lil, you did your best. You did all right with me, and Doreen was never easy, even as a kid. More like her dad than she ever was our side of the family.'

'I expect you're right duck, but I feel it's my last chance to help her now and I want to see her settled down before I kick the bucket.'

'Don't talk like that Lily.' Ellen looked concerned. 'Anyway, I reckon Carol'll jump at the chance. You always were good with her Lily, she liked you better than anyone and she'd listen to you when we could all talk ourselves hoarse. Lil? Lily?' Ellen smiled and put a plump hand on her sleeping sister's bare crepey arm before going into the kitchen for another ginger beer.

Carol arrived at four o'clock. She walked straight out to the garden and kissed her mother and her aunt.

'What you been doing then young Caz?' Lily asked. 'No, don't tell me. I know what I'd have been doing at your age and I wouldn't have told *my* old aunt.'

Carol smiled. 'I've been in the park.' She looked at Lily, mischief in her eyes. 'Lots of nice young men in the park. Very young, about six or seven most of them. It's a holiday play scheme; poor little sods haven't anywhere to go during the day and at least they're safe with us. 'Til they go home at any rate.' She looked down at her heavy black boots as she said this, and flicked at the laces with a ringed and black varnished finger. 'Anyway, how are you Aunt Lily? Mum says you've got a surprise for me; hope it's a good one.'

'Does this job in the park pay you anything?' Carol shook her head. 'Hmm. Well, Carol Marie, what would you say about coming down to stay with me in Cornwall? You'd have somewhere to live and good food and it's at the seaside; bit quiet in the winter for you I expect but plenty going on in the summer. Those hokey cokey bars and things.'

'Karaoke,' Carol said.

'That's what I said, hokey cokey and you'd stand a better chance of finding a job than up here, there's always seasonal work if you keep your eyes and ears open. Are you interested?'

Carol looked at her mother, trying to see what her reaction would be if she decided to go away: then she looked towards Lily who was watching her slyly, happy to see her carefully worked out plan progressing so well. 'I'm buying a house just round the corner from a friend and you could have your own bedsit there. Oh, don't worry, I shan't check up on you. You'd be just like any other lodger, have to pay me rent but I'll do your washing, seeing as it's you.'

'I've heard it's nice in Cornwall. Some friends went down last year and they said it was brilliant.'

'It's lovely my duckie, nicest place I've ever been. Ever so warm and there's the sea and the beaches. You do still like swimming?' Lily imagined the heavy makeup and hair dye being washed away in the sparkling salt sea, leaving exposed the pretty girl who looked after vulnerable children in the park and who reminded her aunt so much of herself as she had been and of the young Lily who still lived somewhere inside the dry, deceptive frame of an old woman.

'Sounds good. Sounds great, but I can't come until the kids go back to school, it wouldn't be fair.'

'I shan't be moving for, oh I don't know, six or eight weeks I suppose, so when you're ready all you've got to do is let me know.'

The sun caught the stud in Carol's nose, making it glisten as she smiled a huge happy grin. 'Thanks Lily. I've got a good feeling about this. I think something brilliant is going to happen.' She unlaced her Doc Marten boots and small pink feet appeared like petals out of an unpromising bud. 'Something really brilliant.'

II

October

The summer which had been so wet and disappointing slid grudgingly into autumn. It was as if it tried to redeem it's failure to please by sending out a pulse of warmth and sunshine, but it was almost too late. The beaches were quiet: the out of season visitors preferred the shelters on the promenade where they sat shielded from the sea breezes, before walking slowly towards one of the cafés which advertised 'Senior Citizens' Lunch Specials'. In the afternoon they would amble in the other direction talking of the crispness of the batter around their fish or the assumed dampness of the mattress on their bed; daughters-in-law who knew nothing of discipline and less of thrift and cooking, and sometimes in low voices of having 'it all taken away, you know, down below.' They would sit with handkerchiefs wrapped around an ice cream cornet, catching drips which fell as fast as holiday confidences from their lips.

Cafés and souvenir shops were closing early and the VACANT signs which appeared in too many windows presaged a winter of anxiety and foregone small pleasures.

Gwen Minto had hardly noticed that the season had been poor: Zion House relied on visitors who came back every year and with the advent of Dixie Davey even before the first of the regulars, Gwen had been busier than ever. Dixie and her mother had seemed quite content to stay in the two small rooms at the top of the house, Lily Beagerie showing no sign of wanting to return to her home in London once her allotted holiday had ended. Indeed, she seemed thoroughly settled into a routine of outings, either alone or with Dixie, and regularly called on Gwen in the afternoon when Dixie was busy with mission work or the weather was particularly inclement.

At first Gwen had been irritated by this intrusion but seeing no way to discourage Lily Beagerie without hurting her feelings, Gwen had made every effort to reconcile herself to the presence of this unlooked for company. As the weeks passed she found her forbearance rewarded and gradually she came to look forward to Lily Beagerie's visits, relaxing with her in a way she thought unsuitable with other, less determined, of her paying guests. Lily had, by default, become a friend.

Now, as the rain and wind which had spoilt the summer turned into a mild and ravishing autumn, Lily and Dixie Davey were getting ready to leave Zion House to move into No. 3, Trewavas Terrace and the Clements would just as soon take over Jericho. Gwen knew that Ralph was happy to be able to stay on and work for them and he had discussed with her his plans to buy a half-share of the market garden with Charlo Clements in due time.

With Carol Byrne to help her in the house Gwen would have more time to herself but there was still, she thought, a great deal to occupy her mind. Ever since Richard Seaton's death nearly a year ago, interlocking pieces of other peoples' lives seemed to have become dislocated like a jigsaw knocked to the floor, the nearly completed picture now fragmented and needing to be reassembled. She wondered what would become of those redundant pieces which no longer fitted into the reconstructed pattern and whether Binnie was doing the right thing by moving to Owles Court. She kept her uncertainty to herself and quashed any gossip she heard about Binnie and James, somehow finding words to convey the truth of their situation without exposing James to further speculation.

Enys Williams, too, would soon be leaving Zion House and Gwen found his defection hard to contemplate. If Gwen had not been so honest with herself she would have been able to shrug off the knowledge that for the first time in her long widowhood she had fallen in love and fallen in love, moreover, with a man young enough to be her son; a gentle, handsome man whose reserve was absolute. Gwen knew herself to be ridiculous; she had hoped never again to feel the disturbance that accompanied her everywhere like some unwanted doppelganger, or to lose the contentment which her life with Ralph afforded her, but as the weeks went by she came to recognise that it was love she felt for Enys Williams, not, as she had hoped, an absurd, untimely infatuation. She was able to laugh with Ralph when he teased her, concealing from him the truth that filled her with astonishment and mortification. The disruption in her life was something she learned to accept, as she would have accepted a debilitating illness or had her hearing failed. It became in time a recollected inconvenience, except when some warm autumn evening brought unexpected restlessness which forced her to turn her thoughts along a more acceptable pathway but which, for a little while, filled her heart with desolation.

And now Enys was leaving to move into Court Farm. Gwen thought about that too: James and Binnie and Enys, forming and reforming in patterns like a kaleidoscope, always the same colours, always falling into a different order. Gwen had watched Ralph reluctantly withdraw support from Binnie, understanding without resentment that his place was being taken by someone with title to be with her; she had watched and been unable to help. Ralph no longer discussed Binnie with his mother and for the first time there was unmapped ground between them. No one else would notice, but Gwen and Ralph knew that things would never be quite the same: a line had been drawn which neither of them would cross.

Lily knocked lightly on the back door of Zion House, no longer a guest but a visitor in her own right. Pearl Angove was sitting in Lily's erstwhile chair facing Gwen, the ever present cups of tea in front of them. Gwen stood up as Lily came into the kitchen and refilled the tea pot from the kettle hissing gently on the back of the stove. 'Find yourself a cup Mrs Beagerie, the tea's still fresh.'

Lily sat down with her back to the heat and studied Pearl's face. 'That looks painful, you want to try some witch hazel. I've got some I'll pop round to you later on.'

Pearl had put a hand to the side of her cheek. 'I walked into a kitchen cabinet, don't know how I didn't notice I'd left it open.'

Lily gave one of her throaty laughs which turned into a cough. 'I used to walk into doors a lot myself at one time but one day a "door" broke two of my ribs,' she paused, then continued in a hard, bright tone, 'and I had a miscarriage on the kitchen floor.' She stopped to drink her tea, only the cup rattling against the saucer as she replaced it giving any indication of her agitation. When she continued her voice was under control and as dispassionate as if she were discussing a scene she had witnessed long ago. 'When I'd scraped myself together a bit I went to look for Doreen and found the poor little mite crouching in a corner of the living room scared half to death, so I threw a change of clothes into a carrier bag and dragged her with me round to my old mum's.

'You don't need to tell me about "doors", I know all about *those* kind of "doors", bastards the lot of them. Came looking for us of course, crying and promising he'd change and I nearly gave in but my old mum might only have been small like me but she saw him off. The language! I'd never heard the like, never even guessed she knew such words, must've picked them up when she lived near Billingsgate as a girl. Scared him off all right, and she got me and Doreen sorted out. No, you don't need to tell me about any "doors".'

Gwen was sitting very still, watching Lily Beagerie, the old woman's face curiously blank, her hands folded into small wrinkled fists as if she were still capable of fighting for her life. Pearl's face had gone very red and then the tide of crimson ebbed, leaving the bruise around her cheek and eye standing out like a thundercloud in a clear sky. She looked more than usually plain but there was something so defeated in her expression that the two women sitting with her in their disparate experience of life, were united in their pity and determination to help.

'You mustn't go back to him this time Pearl. You must come and stay here, there's a room free and we'll sort something out after that.' Gwen was angrier than she could remember being for many years. 'He's nothing but a – a bloody hypocrite and he doesn't deserve to be in charge of a jumble sale, let alone other people's lives.' Gwen so rarely swore that the word 'bloody' was difficult for her to pronounce but Lily Beagerie had no such inhibitions.

'Bastards like him get away with it all the time because no one believes it happens in respectable families: who'd have believed *you* Mrs A. if you'd said your husband was a vicious sod? No one at all, and none of his precious congregation I'll be bound. I'll help you too, Mrs Angove, and pleased to, my duck.'

'*I* knew.' Gwen's voice was quiet. '*I* knew but I didn't know what to do about it. I could have done something but I didn't.'

Pearl looked at her. 'There was nothing you could have done Gwen. You helped by keeping quiet about it, but that's all over now.' Her colour had returned to it's normal unattractive sallow, but the expression on her face had changed to one of resolution. 'There's a funeral this afternoon – old Mr Pedder from the bike shop, you remember him Gwen – and I'll go to that. I'll play for the hymns and while the lilywhite minister goes to the crematorium I'll move my things out.'

Lily Beagerie put out a hand heavy with diamonds. 'You can come to me. I've lots of room and then Mrs M. here won't be stuck for letting rooms. I'll keep you safe: at my age I'm not afraid of bullies and I reckon we'll get on all right. Would you like that?'

Pearl nodded her head just once, the camouflage of embarrassment closing her face to further intrusions.

Matt Pedder's coffin was carried into the chapel as Pearl Angove played softly on the harmonium. She let her fingers drift slowly over the thin, yellowing keys, very conscious that she was doing it for the last time. There was a smell of mothballed wool and spruced up old men in the air behind her. Matt Pedder had been born in a cottage already two centuries old and he had lived and worked in the town all his life. The chapel was full and Pearl listened to her husband's voice recalling for the mourners specious details of Matthew Pedder's pedestrian advancement through life.

Pearl had always played the harmonium at the chapel, dreading more than any other the repercussions of a wedding. It was then, when the Reverend Wilfred came home from his token appearance at a reception in a hired hall or the chapel meeting room, that Pearl had learned to expect violence, the bruises and abrasions inflicted in secret places hidden by her clothing. It was only lately that he had become careless, and Pearl too weary of deception to try and hide the evidence of his perfidy.

The Reverend Wilfred had stopped talking and almost automatically Pearl started to play the opening notes of the Twenty-third Psalm, remembering in time that Matt Pedder had asked for *How Great Thou Art*. Quickly she changed key catching out a few wavering voices and wondering why hymns chosen for funerals were always too high. Only once the chapel had reverberated with beautiful sound, when a male voice choir had sung unaccompanied 'The Old Rugged Cross' for a departed companion, and Pearl had listened with joy in her heart.

She let the music die away as the chapel emptied, the family squashing into big hired Daimlers, the Reverend Wilfred preceding them to Truro in his Simca, rusty as was everyone's car, from the salt-laden air.

As soon as she had locked the chapel door, Pearl crossed the slippery, fern-fringed passage that separated the chapel from the house and started to pack her clothes into a suitcase; there weren't many and she was soon finished. She wandered around the kitchen and the dismal, shabby rooms, filling two shopping bags with everything else that she wanted to take with her and then carried the suitcase to Lily Beagerie's house, careless of anyone watching her progress. When she went back to collect the shopping bags and to walk through the underwater darkness of the rooms where she had pieced out the despair of her marriage, she thought about leaving a note on the hall table where she knew that Wilfred would look for messages as soon as he got home. She decided with satisfying malevolence that it would hurt him more to have to discover her whereabouts by making enquiries among their acquaintances and his parishioners, so she closed the front door for the last time and walked down to the main road and up Trewavas Terrace to where Lily Beagerie was waiting for her.

'Hello Pearl.' The voice wasn't Lily Beagerie's and Pearl looked up as the front door opened. Carol Byrne was standing there and she leaned over to take the heavier of Pearl's bags from her. 'Lily's got the fatted calf in the kitchen and I'll be down for my share when I've taken your bags upstairs.'

Pearl looked with disapproval at the ragged black leggings and the tattooed spider's web just showing where a torn off sleeve only partly covered Carol's pale arm. Pearl's, 'Mrs Angove, if you don't mind,' died before it was born as a hand with glittering black nails lifted the second bag out of her possession.

Carol grinned at her. 'Don't worry Pearl, I shan't run off with your belongings, I'm only going to put them in your bedroom. Go on through, you know the way.' Pearl Angove walked down the passage to the back of the house while Carol ran upstairs, black boots thumping on every tread.

Lily Beagerie had taken possession of Sadie's kitchen just as it was. She liked the way that Sadie had left her mark on it, finding the slightly battered cupboards as cheerful and agreeable as Sadie herself. She had left the red and white gingham café curtains and Lily thought they gave the kitchen a look of French insouciance which she intended to retain.

'I see that Carol's quite at home already. She took my things upstairs for me.' There was a silence, full of unspoken disapproval. 'Called me Pearl, if you please.'

Lily smiled. 'She calls everyone by their first name. I rather like it; when you get to my age there's hardly anyone left to call you by your Christian name and it makes me feel old to be Mrs Beagerie all the time. You can call me Lily if you like, and don't you worry about Carol, she's as true as a bell and got more sense than most people you'd meet in a day's march.'

Pearl sat down and looked around her. 'I suppose you'll have to decorate the whole house once you've settled. I don't mean to be rude Mrs B – Lily, but it could do with a bit of touching up couldn't it?'

Lily pushed a teacup towards Pearl. 'Tell you what duck, you can do whatever you like with your room but, do you know, I like the house like this, makes it feel as if a real family lives here. My house has always been a bit too tidy and quiet for me because that's the way Doreen liked it, but now with young Carol around bringing a bit of life into the place, I think I'll just leave it as it is.'

Carol appeared and looked for orange juice in the fridge. 'All right Pearl? You've got the best room you know. I *begged* Lily to let me have it but she said it was for you and it would be wasted on me.' She gave her aunt a smile. 'I don't mind really, I reckon you deserve a bit of spoiling.' She looked at Pearl, eyes like a marmoset's looking seriously out of the mask of make-up. 'I think you're really brave: we both do, don't we Lily? You're not to worry about that hypocritical old sod finding you, Lily and I are more than a match for him and we're going to make sure you have a bit of fun from now on. We're both good at fun aren't we Lily?' Carol piled peanut butter on a slice of bread, sweeping the crumbs on to the floor before wandering towards the back door. 'Got to go, I'm collecting Hannah from Holy Joe's so that Cora can help Sadie and then I think that Ralph's going to take us to Newlyn to watch the fish being unloaded, Hannah enjoys that.' She turned around. 'I'm really glad you're here Pearl. See you later.'

Lily looked at Pearl. She had been going to reassure her

but instead she held tightly to the worn and dry hand of the woman opposite her. 'It's all right my duck, you cry all you want, you'll feel better in a while. The worst bit's over; there, there, Pearl duckie.' She comforted her with ingenuous words, remembered from a time long ago when life had been simple and all she had to do was to soothe the sting of a grazed knee and kiss the pain better. Carol was right, Lily thought, she *was* glad to have Pearl with her, prejudiced and sarcastic as she knew her to be. It was the new beginning she had so carefully engineered: Pearl, Carol and Doreen, all of them still only vaguely aware of the opportunities that Lily Beagerie saw so clearly.

'Leave your lists and come to Court Farm with me. I need advice and the garden can wait a bit longer.' Enys leaned over the table and spoke to Binnie, his face only just not touching hers. She looked down and added, 'Plant irises and bulbs – ?agapanthus,' to the pad of paper in front of her. It was covered in writing: 'Returfing. Trim hedges. ?Vine. <u>Remove dahlias</u>. Pick pears. Rose beds. Ask James about coppicing. Bamboo.'

'What advice can I give you, you know about furniture and how you want the house to look. If,' she said, 'what you really meant to say was, "Come and have lunch with me Binnie," then I would feel inclined to do so.' Binnie yawned and pushed the pad away from her, satisfied with her morning's work. James had walked the gardens with her and together they had agreed on what was to be done.

'I've always so disliked dahlias, James, may I dig them up?'

'Do what you like my dear. The only thing that I must ask you to spare is the yellow rose in the hedge of the sunken garden, it's my great favourite. I always feel there must be some reason why I'm so fond of it, but if there is, then my memory of it is gone.'

James was looking better than he had for some months and Binnie's anxiety about him had lessened. The wing of the house she was to live in had so far shown no sign of attention from a builder but for the time being Binnie was quite comfortable as James' guest. The house ran smoothly without her having to do anything, the food was excellent and James circumspect in his appropriation of Binnie's time. When she asked him about the plans for the rooms which they had agreed would be hers, he reassured her that he had to wait for the right builder to be free and that work would start quite soon.

Enys tried again. 'Come and have lunch with me Binnie.'

'Sorry Enys, I was just thinking about James. Where shall we go?'

'I thought a picnic?'

'Oh, good, you always have such lovely ideas. Meet you outside in five minutes.' Binnie kissed his cheek and then stood smiling at him. 'I did that without thinking,' she said, and added in a deliberate way, 'just as if we were young again,' before she left him standing by the round library table while she went to find her jacket.

'This wasn't a planned excursion so the food's a bit odd. I've just got bits and pieces out of the kitchen. What do you think?'

Binnie was sitting on a bench of slatted wood that encircled the trunk of an oak, having looked carefully to find somewhere to sit down that wasn't obviously under a bird's roost. Enys put down a cardboard box in which were a loaf of bread and a plastic tub of butter. There was one fillet of smoked mackerel and a piece of cheese, a jar of peanut butter and some grapes.

'Looks yummy, as Katha would say.' Binnie started to giggle.

'Oh Binnie I haven't heard you laugh like that for so

long.' Enys was looking at her in the way she remembered and she felt herself beginning to blush.

'Drinks?'

'Damn. I forgot.' Enys disappeared and came back with a bottle of mineral water and two mugs and they started to eat their odd little picnic, not talking very much, not looking at each other at all. When they had finished and could no longer pretend to be occupied there was a silence until Enys said in a voice that sounded loud in the basking garden, 'This all feels so *déjà vu* that I half expect Richard to come around the corner and tell me that it's his turn to take you out.'

'Richard.' Binnie turned her head to look at Enys. 'Do you miss him?'

'I miss his lightheartedness and the way he never bore grudges, but I can't forgive him for what he did to you. Or perhaps it's that I can't forgive myself, what do you think?'

Binnie sat upright so abruptly that it startled Enys. 'One thing I must say, Enys,' she looked fiercely at him, 'Richard is dead. Dead. And I don't want you, or us, or anyone, to keep on talking about him.'

'But you asked me . . .'

'I know, and I regretted it at once. We both know what he was like and in spite of all that, he did love Jory and I believe he tried to do his best for us. At least for a while. Until it got boring. He could never stand being bored, you know.' There was another, longer silence until Binnie said, 'I didn't mean any of that. I only started talking about Richard because I thought you were going to talk about us.'

'You don't think we should talk about us then? I rather felt we should and I hoped that you did.'

'What's there to talk about? We can't go back twenty years Enys, everything's changed.'

'Not everything.'

Sunlight was trickling through the branches of the tree, dappling the grey, cracked wood of the garden bench and as it crept across Binnie's feet, bleaching her old, worn espadrilles, she remembered the summer of plane tree shadows on hot London pavements, of gaudy, gauzy dresses and mirrored skirts and she looked at Enys, older and handsomer and much sadder and she knew that she loved him as he was now, no less than she had loved him then.

'No, not everything.' She smiled at him, the beautiful topaz eyes filled with shared secrets as she leaned her head against his shoulder. Japanese anemones were lambent candelabra on the edge of Binnie's vision and she thought that so much had been spoilt by the rain this year that these late opening flowers seemed more welcome than ever as they shone against grass which was thick and as green as in a seedsman's catalogue. Enys put his arm around her and she felt the worn, corded softness of his old trousers under her palm.

Much later they walked hand in hand through the empty rooms of the farmhouse. 'It doesn't look as if anything's been done to it for years. Look at that lino!' Linoleum was laid on the floor of the small bedrooms at the top of the house, flowers so smudged with wear that Enys and Binnie could see exactly where the bed had been, a pathway to the door clearly marked through the imitation parquet tiles which edged the flowered pattern. Another unfaded square showed where it must have been covered by a wash stand or a chest of drawers under the window. A curtain trailed from a wire which was fixed to the edge of a triangular piece of wood nailed across a corner of the room to form a hanging cupboard.

'Look at the nails!' Binnie pulled a piece of rusting metal from one of the dark wooden beams, and another, and another, from wood and plaster until they both had hands full of them and they leant against the whitewashed wall laughing with the pleasure of each other's company.

'It seems a shame to have to spoil it all don't you think? Perhaps we could open it to the public as a rural museum.'

'And then where would you live? Simla?'

Enys looked at Binnie, hair untidy, face relaxed and rosy with laughter. 'I could come and live with you.'

'If James' builder doesn't get a move on I might have to come and live with *you*.'

'I knew you'd get there in the end.'

'What do you mean? Get where?'

'Have you ever known James not to do what he says he will? Hasn't it occurred to you that this builder's job on the Cathedral is very convenient, always almost finished but not quite yet?'

'You mean,' Binnie said slowly, 'that getting me to move to Owles Court was a – a ruse? That James doesn't really want me to live there at all – and what about the garden? I'm sure he's serious about the garden.'

'Of course he is and I'm sure he was sincere when he asked you to live in the house, but d'you remember how I told you that James seems to know what people want before they know it themselves?' Binnie nodded, but standing in that old-fashioned room and feeling alive and happy for the first time for months, she suddenly realised that she didn't understand at all. Enys went on, 'You can work on the gardens just as easily from here and I shall have somewhere as a base for my antiques. There's all the room I could possibly need in the stables and I could even have a workshop out there. Are you beginning to understand?'

'But if James wants me to live here why did he offer it to you?'

'Because he knows that we love each other and because

he understood at once that you might be reluctant to marry me so soon after, you know, the thing I'm not allowed to mention, but this way it just seems much easier, that's all.'

Binnie looked at her hands full of rusty nails and then she looked at Enys. 'You've never said that before. You never once said that you loved me, do you know that?' She put the nails on the window sill and as she turned, her arm caught the dirty green curtain. Dust showered out of it's ragged folds and Binnie looked at it as if she needed to remember for ever the pattern of wheatsheaves and poppies placed geometrically on the material. The dye of the poppies seemed particularly destructive and a hole had formed at each red flower head.

'Why didn't you tell me about Jory? You must have known I'd know for certain as soon as I saw him.'

'Because I knew that if you'd married me you'd have left the army and I knew how much it meant to you. Richard didn't seem to mind: he really didn't Enys, or I wouldn't have married him.'

'Of course Richard didn't mind: I minded though but I didn't find it strange. After all, Jory could have been his child.' Enys took Binnie's hand and together they walked down the twisting stairs, each remembering to duck under the heavy beam that formed the top of the doorway.

'It's still warm, come and sit outside,' he said and they passed the oak tree where they'd had their picnic and walked to where a cast iron seat seemed planted in a meadow of long grass. The sun was behind them and their shadows were beginning to stretch thinly along the ground.

They sat silently for a while, then Binnie said, 'Richard always accepted that he might have been Jory's father and by the time he realised that he wasn't, it had stopped being of any importance.' There were blistered bubbles of paint on the iron seat and Binnie burst them with her fingernail one after the other, as she said this. 'I always thought, you see, that it was very brave of him to take me on and I didn't make much fuss about, well, the bad bits because I was so grateful to him. It was a *kind* of love, wasn't it?'

'I suppose it was.' Enys didn't look at Binnie's pale face. 'Richard knew that James was very unlikely to have a child and he was funny about keeping the house in the family. It was terribly important to him and I think he saw it as his duty to provide an heir. I do think he just took the opportunity when it presented itself and, as things turned out, it was the best thing he could have done.'

'But why shouldn't James have children? Oh, I know he's not well now but he's getting stronger again and he's only a few years older than us.'

'Katha wouldn't have had to ask that.' He paused. 'Do you really not know, Binnie?' Binnie shook her head and Enys continued, 'Why do you think that James has never married?' Enys was looking at her, the question and the answer to it in his eyes. 'That's why he discouraged you and Richard from living with him, he was afraid you might not approve.'

'I see: of course I can see now that you tell me. And you mean Katha knows about James?'

Enys nodded. 'She probably knows about Jory too, have you thought of that?'

'Not Katha! She *can't* know, she'd have said something, you know she can't keep anything to herself.'

Enys looked steadily at Binnie. 'I don't think that's so Binnie, Katha can be very secretive when she wants to be. The person who really can't keep anything to herself is Pammie Brighton. She seemed to enjoy hinting to me that she'd seen Katha in out-of-the-way places with men other than Casey. Odd, really, when you know her own reputation.'

Binnie thought about telling Enys that Pammie was going to marry Brooke Olver and what James had said about him but instead she just said, 'Bitch,' remembering at the same time the shock of discovering how little she, herself, had really known about Katha. There was, too, at the back of Binnie's mind, a feeling she was trying to ignore and which she wished to conceal from Enys. She was afraid he wouldn't understand the gratification she felt at the thought that Pammie Brighton was about to get her just deserts.

'So she is, but I suspect that Katha managed to keep most of that side of her life quiet, or am I wrong?'

'You're right, of course. I never suspected anything Enys, not for all these years and then, when she asked me for help, I refused. Disapproving again you see. James is right, I *am* self righteous.'

'He didn't say that and I don't think that you are. You just see things in a very black and white way – and perhaps it's a good thing that someone still does.'

'I suppose,' Binnie was thinking aloud, 'that I just accepted what I was taught by Uncle Basil and Aunt Vee. They were so good to me that it was much easier not to question their beliefs and now I don't know if I believe any of it any more or whether it's just habit carrying on as I've always done.'

Binnie was still picking at shreds and blisters of old green paint and she went on, 'Do you remember when we met in London and how disapproving I was of the way my Flinders cousins lived? I'm surprised really that you bothered with me at all.'

'It wasn't just you, everyone disapproved of the way the Flinders lived. Who'd guess to see Tom on his feet in the House of Commons these days that he was one of the biggest hellraisers in our circle. And Bella with what, four children and a house in Gloucestershire?'

'Six children, and it's Hampshire, she's even grander these days.'

They both laughed, relaxing into their familiar easiness with each other. A light breeze had sprung up and was blowing across the long grass. In the evening light it looked like the pelt of some magical animal.

'Enys, what am I going to do about James?'

'My dear, darling Binnie, nothing. Absolutely nothing, everything's just the same as far as he's concerned. What you really need to think about is what you're going to do about *me*.'

Enys was leaning back against the peeling paintwork of the seat, long legs stretched out in front of him, hands in his pockets and all the remote watchfulness of a few months ago had disappeared. After a while, when Binnie had not answered him, he turned his head towards her and smiled his sweet, young man's smile. 'Will you marry me?'

Binnie nodded, not able to speak, and Enys wrapped his arms around her. They stayed together in the garden until their shadows merged into one shadow and was taken captive by the night.

12

November

From the larger greenhouse Ralph was able to see when Carol and Hannah turned in at Jericho's gate. Several times a week, when Cora was helping Sadie in the house, Carol went to St Joseph's to collect Hannah and Ralph had fallen into the habit of waiting for them, strolling across their path as if by chance, walking with them into the kitchen, sitting with them while they talked and picked at biscuits. Sometimes he managed to be occupied in the house and needing a hand with some task when the two young women arrived home and Carol would encourage Hannah to help them, talking to her as if she accepted that Hannah understood everything that was said to her.

Ralph watched all this and he knew Carol's worth. Lily had sent her to Zion House one Saturday morning when Ralph and Gwen had been lingering over breakfast. Usually Saturday was one of the busiest days of the week but Zion House had been quiet, the three long term guests all having left at once and the next group of visitors not due for a week. Ralph was looking at a brochure of Aids for the Disabled which had arrived tucked inside the *Radio Times* and which reminded him that the next booking he and his mother were expecting were all pensioners and that always meant extra washing and special diets. The loudness of the front door bell startled them both.

'Bit early for front door callers.' Gwen looked up. 'See who it is, there's a dear.'

Ralph had opened the door, holding it tightly as a wind scudding around the corner of the house fought to tear it from his hands. Carol Byrne stood on the step, neat and clean but dressed from head to foot in black. What hair she had was black and her eyes looked out of black sockets. She was wearing a black leather jacket and a black cotton skirt that just skimmed her bottom, leaving what seemed to be yards of black legs to descend to Doc Marten's.

Ralph looked at her and saw none of this. He noticed that she was dressed in something unbecoming but what he saw was a girl with a mouth like an Ena Harkness rose and clever grey eyes.

'I'm Caz. Hi! I've come to see Mrs Minto and I expect you're Ralph, aren't you? Can I come in, it's blowing a hooligan out here?'

'Of course, of course, sorry, come in. Mother's in the kitchen. We're a bit behind this morning, I'm afraid.' Ralph had stood aside to let Carol Byrne into the house and as she passed him he could smell very faintly something sweet and musky that seemed to come from her clothes. 'Let me show you the way,' and Ralph had walked down the passage to the kitchen, cannoning off the serving table against the wall, as he seemed unable to take his eyes off her for long enough to see where he was going.

'Caz Byrne, Mother.' Gwen had looked up as Ralph held the door open and Carol Byrne had walked into the kitchen and unassailably into their lives.

'Hello, Mrs Minto. Aunt Lily said you might have a job

for me, so I thought I'd come and see if there's anything I can do.'

'Your aunt's quite right Caz, I do need someone to help me here in the house, but do you think it would suit you?' Gwen's eyes flickered over the small, eccentric figure, and she reminded herself not to judge by appearances. 'Would you like a cup of tea?'

'No thanks but I'll have some orange juice if you've got any.'

Ralph had opened the fridge door and was pouring out a glass of juice almost before Carol had finished speaking. Gwen looked at him, attuned to his every mood. Over the years Ralph's romantic attentions had been focused on several young women but none had stayed the course. Now, in this fantastic little figure dressed like a child in a Halloween costume, and standing in her kitchen talking away as if they were old friends, Gwen knew quite surely that she had met the opponent who would eventually vanquish her.

'Sit down for a minute and I'll tell you what the job entails. I'm not sure what your aunt has told you Caz,' Gwen looked at her speculatively, 'but I need someone to give me a hand with the day-to-day work; changing the beds, preparing vegetables, cleaning the bathrooms, all those sort of jobs.'

'Sounds all right to me. I'm very strong Mrs Minto and I can do all that. I can use a word processor and do book keeping too, and I'm a good cook. A real little treasure in fact.' Carol smiled at Gwen as she said this but Gwen was perfectly aware of the resolution that was only lightly covered by Carol's flippancy.

In the weeks that followed Carol Byrne's arrival at Zion House, Gwen wondered many times why it was sometimes easier to make allowances for the perverse and the difficult than to accept what someone as cheerful and conscientious as Carol had to offer. Carol was as good as her word, the house ran as smoothly as it had always done in spite of Gwen being relieved of drudgery and it quickly became apparent that Carol was popular with the older guests who stayed at Zion House at the cheaper end of the season. The only thing that Gwen felt she had to ask her to do was to remove her black nail varnish.

'It looks so queer alongside the fried eggs in the morning, offputting to say the least,' she had said to Ralph over dinner one evening and Ralph had shrugged, unwilling to join in any criticism of Carol, who now occupied his thoughts all day and caused him to lie awake on many nights thinking of her: of how her tattooed arms reached palely across the laundered sheets as she made the beds and how he longed to touch the docked hair on her head to see if it was sharp like bristles or downy and silken like velvet, but most of all it was Carol's soft, crimson mouth that he saw in the darkness behind his eyes.

Ralph's work at Jericho became only the intervals of time between his being able to see Carol and if she seemed unaware of his interest there were observers who noticed how often she went to see if Sadie needed help or to take Hannah to visit the house when Cora was working there.

Jericho was being altered in accordance with its new role as a private hotel. Over the winter two new bathrooms would be installed and a shower and washbasin fitted in every bedroom. Sadie thought Binnie's choice of colours drab and insipid and only Charlo's repeated financial cautioning persuaded her that they should not undertake major redecorating until the business was established. Sadie had insisted however, on livening up the entrance hall and cloakroom. Where once there had been a jumble of old, shabby coats and walking sticks and where Richard's beautiful riding boots had consorted with assorted, unpaired wellingtons, she and Cora were painting the walls a warm, welcoming yellow. In the fireplace which dominated the hall, Sadie intended to have a log fire for the winter and an arrangement of dried flowers and grasses in a basket during the summer. She had bought a large, mahogany table from Binnie and this would be used as a desk along the wall behind the front door. Sadie thought copper ornaments and pictures by local artists would complete the arrangement she had in her mind's eye and she intended to ask Enys Williams to look out for them for her at auction.

If most people had been taken aback by the announcement of a marriage between Enys Williams and Binnie Seaton, Sadie was perhaps only mildly surprised. She had watched Binnie relaxing and unfurling like a flower in the months that Enys had spent in Zion House and she wondered how far Binnie's increasing contentment had influenced her in accepting their offer to buy Jericho, for Sadie was aware that it had been a very advantageous deal as far as they were concerned. Now Sadie's astute observation was again engaged, this time in watching Ralph's infatuation for Carol Byrne deepen and develop and she hoped with all her kind heart that this time Ralph would persevere, for she thought them well suited.

As Sadie and Cora finished painting another wall of the hall, they sat on the bottom step of the staircase, which curved away above their heads three storeys high to the rooms where Sadie and Charlo would live. Cora lit a cigarette and Sadie started to chat. 'That little Caz's made all the difference to you, you know Cora. You look better and much more relaxed because you know Hannah's safe with her, and Hannah's obviously taken to her, the dear of her. Where are they going now – Newlyn?' Cora nodded and let her thoughts drift, listening to Sadie with enough attention to reply in the right places to her questions.

'I tell you another person who's taken with her, and that's Ralph. Have you noticed how he can hardly keep his eyes off her? I'd never have believed it, thought he was firmly tied to the apron strings. Not that there's anything wrong with that, mind you, and I wouldn't say a word against Gwen Minto, she's a really lovely person, but I really did think that Ralph was too set in his ways to change. What do you think Cora? Would you have thought he'd ever get married?'

Cora looked for somewhere to put out her cigarette and went into the empty, newly painted cloakroom, dropping the stub into the lavatory bowl before rejoining Sadie on the stairs. She looked with affection at her friend. 'I don't know Sadie, you understand people much better than I do but, yes, I think Ralph and Carol would make a good match although he's a lot older than her, isn't he?' She rubbed her paint flecked hands together and then said, 'Young Jory seems very taken with her too, what does Jassy think of that?'

'Do Jassy good to see that Jory's not so devoted to her that she can walk all over him. Even though she's my own daughter I know what she's like and now that she's seen Jory looking at someone else, she's gone all keen on him.' Sadie laughed and looked at Cora, her face fading into placidity once more. 'Sometimes I feel I shouldn't talk to you so much about Jassy, but you're so understanding Cora and I do need to sometimes, and then I think that *you've* got no one to talk to and I know it isn't always easy for you – money and things I mean.' She stopped and Cora put down the cigarette she had just lit. She had found an empty paint tin and was using the lid as an ashtray.

'I manage Sadie, I always have.' She prodded the skin of yellow paint with a matchstick. 'We've known each other a long time, haven't we?' Sadie nodded, eyes on Cora's face. 'You've often hinted at things but you've never asked me outright about Hannah or her father and I know that's been difficult for you. No, don't be cross,' she put out a placating hand to Sadie, 'it's because I trust you that I'm going to tell you now.' The cigarette had gone out and Cora relit it, her hands shaking slightly. 'Hannah,' she stopped and was silent for so long that Sadie thought that she had changed her mind, but she waited, sitting quite still, and eventually Cora said again, 'Hannah. Sadie, Hannah isn't my own child.' The silence in the hall was so complete that they could hear Ralph and Carol and Hannah in the kitchen, laughing and talking together.

'Hannah's parents were professional people; her father was a barrister and her mother a violinist – and I was Hannah's nanny. She was a beautiful baby, good and quiet, and her parents thought that all babies were like that but I realised after a while that she was *too* quiet and she wasn't developing as she should. I tried to tell them that something was wrong but they couldn't, or wouldn't, understand.' Cora's voice sounded tense and high. 'We were living in Scotland in a Gothic horror miles from anywhere so it wasn't difficult to keep Hannah away from other people but when she was eighteen months old her mother became pregnant again.' Cora stopped. 'I've never spoken about this to anyone Sadie, not in twenty years.'

'You know I'll never tell anyone, not even Charlo.'

'I know.' There were splashes of paint on the tiles of the floor and they seemed important to Cora but she made herself look away from them and went on with her story. 'Hannah's mother was what is called "highly strung" – I always thought that funny for someone who played the violin – and suddenly she couldn't bear to have Hannah near her. She wouldn't talk to her or touch her, she wouldn't even look at her most of the time. I suppose she thought it might influence the new baby; I really don't know because I could never understand it.' Cora sat thinking of the hysterical outbursts that had tainted the days of twenty years ago, of the tears and tantrums from which she had tried to shield the little girl. 'Hannah's father did what he could but he was in Edinburgh all the week and came home to scenes every weekend and he soon got fed up with it.'

Sadie sat without saying a word, hoping that Charlo wouldn't be back from the Tec. too early as she felt sure that Cora, once interrupted, would never continue.

'I can hardly remember now whether it was him or me who thought of it, but all of a sudden we seemed to be talking about me taking Hannah away and her parents saying that she had died.'

Sadie couldn't keep quiet altogether. 'What about her grandparents, Cora, wouldn't they be suspicious?'

'Only her father's parents were alive and I think they probably just assumed that Hannah had been put into an institution and that it was better to forget her. Some people are like that you know.' Cora looked at Sadie, whose face was full of disbelief. 'It's true, Sadie, not everyone is like you, or like me for that matter, and it was,' she said grimly, 'easier just to "lose" Hannah. That's it really.' Cora's voice had returned almost to normal. 'Hannah's father bought us our house, as far away as possible from his home, and twice a year he sends me money for her. It's still the same amount we agreed on twenty years ago so it's not a great deal of help, but better than nothing and I've always managed.'

'Cora, I had no idea. I thought that Hannah was probably illegitimate or that you were divorced – haven't you ever been married?' Sadie's soft brown eyes were sad, her mouth set in a line of reproach of such cruelty.

Cora shook her head. 'Not even tempted. Hannah has been my whole life,' she said quietly, 'there's been no room for anyone else, but I've never regretted it, not for a minute.'

'Haven't you worried about her parents wanting to see her?'

'I did wonder if her father would get in touch this year when she was twenty-one but I just got the usual payment sent from Edinburgh; no letter, just the money.'

'That brown paper package I saw on the table!'

'That's the one. And now you know all my guilty secrets.'

There was sudden, louder laughter from the kitchen and Charlo Clements walked through into the hall. 'Slacking again. Every time I come home, you're sitting down and you say you've been working all day and it's the first time you've stopped.' He kissed Sadie and looked around. 'I like the colour, very cheerful. Oh, by the way,' he turned to Cora, 'Ralph and Carol have taken Hannah out. I said I'd tell you.' He looked at the friends sitting companionably on the bottom of the stairs. 'Do I smell romance in the air?'

'More like paint fumes . . .'

'. . . and cigarette smoke.'

They laughed and pushed themselves up and went to wash their stiffening paintbrushes before Charlo could remind them to do so.

Ralph and Carol drove Hannah back to Trewavas Terrace and sat watching while she climbed the granite steps to No. 2 and rang the bell. Cora had wondered about allowing Hannah to have a key to the front door but had decided it was safer for her not to have unrestricted access to the house. Hannah trusted everyone and her gentle face and long hair like black silk floss attracted attention wherever she went. Cora guarded her as if she were still a precious small child to be protected from harm until she had learned to deal with the world, but for Hannah there would never come a time when Cora's vigilance could be lessened, when she could allow her to wander freely knowing that no one would take advantage of her childlike nature or tear brutally from her the innocence which Cora sought to preserve.

There was no one to whom Cora could relinquish Hannah for more than a few hours: the time she spent at St Joseph's every day was Cora's breathing space, the time when she could earn some money knowing that Hannah was safe and was being well looked after. Hannah made no objection to staying with Sadie or Gwen and she liked Ralph very much but it was Carol whom Hannah had come to love. Carol had treated her from the first with a firm offhandedness that Cora would never have tried and she was astonished to see how Hannah responded, trying to keep up with Carol, using newly learned words and even, occasionally, dancing in odd rythmic patterns, round and round, laughing when she fell over her feet.

Sometimes, still, Cora thought of the little hoard of pills and the syringe kept in a locked attaché case at the bottom of the wardrobe. She had started saving tablets once when she had been ill and she had seen Hannah's distress, knowing something was wrong but unable to understand why Cora lay on the sofa and why Sadie had washed and ironed their clothes and had cooked Hannah her tea each evening. Cora felt as if it had been a dress rehearsal for what might eventually happen to them and she had determined on a plan which would prevent Hannah being exposed to loss and further bewilderment.

After dropping Hannah, Ralph had passed Zion House and had driven far along the promenade, parking in a pool of darkness between two street lights, but he made no move to get out of the car. Carol looked at him and then, putting her hand with its newly naked pink nails on his arm she said, 'In addition to all my other talents I'm a good listener; can't you tell me what's the matter Ralph?

You seemed quite happy earlier on but now you've gone all quiet on me.'

Ralph was holding the steering wheel as if he was about to drive away but he turned his head towards Carol. 'It's all right when we've got Hannah with us but,' he stopped and then took a deep breath, 'I'm so much older than you, and you must know how I feel about you. It seems wrong somehow: you should be out with someone of your own age and I shouldn't even think about you in the way I do. I want to change you, you see; get rid of that awful makeup and let everyone see how pretty you are and I know that isn't right, you should look just as you want to.'

Her eyes half closed as she looked at him in astonishment. 'What about my makeup?'

'I don't like it.' He waited for Carol's 'tough', but instead she unzipped the front of her black leather jacket, Ralph watching the silver teeth peel open, and flinching as Carol threw the jacket onto the seat behind them.

'What don't you like?'

Ralph touched her cheek and held out his hand, pale foundation greasy on his fingers. Carol leaned towards him and wriggled her hand into his trouser pocket, her eyes never leaving his face. She pulled out the clean white handkerchief that Gwen had ironed for him and screwing a corner into a little tassel, she put it into her mouth. Her grey eyes were watching Ralph as she pulled the handkerchief from her mouth and sucked it again to make sure it was wet enough, and then she began to dab at the skin around her eyes, folding and wetting more of the handkerchief until all that was left was a faint black shadow like a fading bruise.

'Satisfied? Will you do the rest for me?' Carol sucked at the handkerchief again and handed it to Ralph. She turned towards him so that he could start on her cheeks. He was terribly aware of Carol's small pink tongue so close to his face but he had hardly started on his task before she kissed him, her pale, strong arms around him and her mouth as soft and sweet as he had always known it would be.

As they moved away from each other Carol giggled. 'You didn't have to say that you don't like my makeup, you could just have kissed me you know. No one's going to say you're a naughty boy or tell on you.'

Ralph was looking over Carol's shoulder and in the light of the lamp nearest to them he saw the familiar crablike movement as a figure moved away from them. 'If you'd lived here a bit longer you wouldn't say that; there's something called the Cornish Underground, no one from outside knows how it works but you sneeze in Penzance and they know in Truro that you've got a cold. Mother'll know by morning what we're up to.'

'We're hardly up to anything – and in any case your mother already knows.'

'Mother knows what?' Ralph was surprised and delighted to see Carol's cheeks becoming pink and shyness invading the black rimmed eyes.

'Well, the way you keep staring at me, she must know that you like me, that's all I meant.'

'Oh, I thought you might have meant that she knows that I'm madly in love with you and that I intend to marry you.'

'Of course that's what I really meant.' She kissed his cheek and Ralph smiled to himself, turning towards her, his hands telling him that Carol's hair was as soft as feathers and he knew it would be beautiful when he had persuaded her to let it grow.

When Carol let herself in at the back door of No. 3, Trewavas Terrace she heard that the television was still on and found her aunt asleep in the brown Dralon-covered chair, bombarded by an old black and white film. Carol touched Lily Beagerie on the shoulder and switched off the television. When she turned around she was startled to see Lily looking at her, wide awake and curious.

'Sit down and talk to me for a bit, duck. You've been out with Ralph again haven't you?'

Carol sat down on a chair which matched her aunt's. 'Yes, we took Hannah to see the fish being unloaded and then Ralph and I went for a drive.'

'Go far?'

'Not very. We talked for a bit, then bought some fish and chips. Oh, and we saw Dixie down by the post office but she didn't see us, she seemed to be in a hurry so we didn't stop. Ralph's just brought me home.'

'You like him don't you, duck?' Carol smiled. 'No need to ask if he likes you, stands out a mile. I've often seen that happen, a man you don't think's interested in getting married at all and then it hits him and he's all over the place like some dopey, love struck kid.'

'Ralph's not dopey, he's really nice Lily; nicer than anyone else I've been out with. He's so kind and he understands all sorts of things you wouldn't expect him to.'

'Living with his mother's done that and always being at the beck and call of that Binnie Seaton. He's a good bit older than you—'

'– only fifteen years, that's not so much.'

'Well, I've always thought it would take someone out of the ordinary to please you Carol Marie and perhaps someone older and settled is what you need. Do you love him?'

'I think so. I'm almost sure I do but you needn't worry, I shan't rush into anything. He's talking about getting married and us eventually running Zion House together, but I've told him he's got to wait, that we don't know each other well enough yet and I've got to be sure. Anyway, I don't want to get married for ages because I've had an idea. Do you want to hear what it is?'

Lily was rubbing her hands over the arms of the chair, a habit which was already causing the velvet to flatten and become thin, and now she nodded to Carol to go on. 'I thought – well, I thought I might train to work with people like Hannah. It's not something I'd ever have thought of doing but I get on really well with Hannah. And it's not just her; sometimes when I go to collect her from Holy Joe's, they let me talk to other people there and I really like them Lily, and I seem to be able to get through to them and it would be something worthwhile to do, wouldn't it?'

Lily put her hand, heavy with diamonds, on Carol's small hand. 'I knew you'd find your feet if you got away from London for a bit. I don't know why your mother ever worried about you, you've got more sense than most people twice your age.'

Carol was looking at the rings on her aunt's thin fingers and then she said hesitantly, 'Lily, could I ask you something?'

'Ask away, my duck.'

'Your rings: they're real diamonds aren't they? They must be worth a lot of money, but—'

'How could I afford them?'

'Well, yes.'

Lily leaned back in the ugly brown chair and looked at Carol. 'I wouldn't tell everyone this and most of them probably think they're the wages of sin anyway, except they don't seem to hold with sin any more these days, but my rings,' she smoothed the big stones and turned her hands so that they shimmered in the light, 'well, they're a reminder to me of someone I knew long ago.' Lily sighed. 'Perhaps that's why I understand how you feel about Ralph. He's not what you'd call the answer to a maiden's prayer but I can see that he suits you and that's all that matters when all's said and done.

'Doreen and me had a difficult time you know, when I left her dad and went to live back at my mother's. I'd taken nothing but a change of clothes and I wasn't very well and Doreen, poor little kiddie, I suppose she was a bit disturbed by all the goings on she'd seen. You know what I'm talking about?' She said this more sharply than she had intended.

Carol didn't seem to notice and said, 'Mum told me that your husband used to beat you up, is that what you mean?'

'Yes, and the rest. The war was on, raids every night, never knowing if you'd still have a home in the morning. Still, you don't want to hear about all that,' Lily said, 'you want to hear about my jewels. I couldn't stay at my mum's for ever so she found us a couple of rooms near her and I took Doreen to live there. I got her into school and I had to earn some money to keep us so I did all sorts. I was on the buses 'til the war ended and then I worked for a butcher for a while, turned my stomach that did; and then in a laundry which was a bit better but I never really liked it there – bad for my chest you see, and then one day I was walking past the pawnbroker's – and I don't know to this day why I did it – but I went in and asked him if he had a job going.' Lily Beagerie was smiling, remembering one of the happier times of her life, her mind full of the dusty, dark shop and the smell of old clothes and poverty to which she became inured. 'I'd been in there once or twice, we all had to pawn things and there was no shame in it, so I knew Sammy Greene a bit by sight.' Lily's face was alight as she looked at Carol. 'He was a funny looking little chap, not much taller than me, round shouldered, and he had a long, grey beard. He wore glasses, round gold ones like all the youngsters wear today. Makes me laugh to see them wearing Sammy's specs and thinking themselves so smart, and he had such eyes! Dark as treacle and always twinkling.

'Anyway, he said he did have a job and if I wanted it, it was mine.' Lily sat silently for a few minutes. 'One of those things I've never understood, how I just went in and asked, just as if I *had* to.

'I worked there for years, until my dear old Sammy died.' She turned to the girl, 'D'you know duckie, he was one of the few good men I've ever met; I don't think most of them are worth the air they breathe, I learned a lot about them in Sammy's shop I can tell you, and you look at that bloody old hypocrite round the corner at the chapel, but Sammy treated me as if I was someone.'

'Did you love him Lily?'

'Oh yes my duck, I did, and we both knew it but we never spoke about it or made anything of it; you didn't in those days and it wouldn't have done you see, him being a Jew, but every so often when there was what we called an unredeemed pledge Sammy would tell me to buy it and he charged me next to nothing.'

'That's where your rings came from?'

'It is, all unredeemed pledges. And that wasn't the end of it. When Sammy died he left me enough money for me to buy my first small house.' Lily Beagerie's eyes shone with tears and she looked round for her dark glasses. Carol moved across and put her arms around the old woman's shoulders: she felt as fragile as a bird and Carol suddenly felt a terrible anguish as she saw her own mortality.

'Oh Lily, what a lovely story.'

'Carol,' her aunt said slowly, 'Doreen isn't really interested in all that old stuff. She thinks it's best forgotten so I wouldn't say anything to her.'

'Oh I shan't but I'm glad you told me. Goodnight Lily.' Carol kissed her aunt and the two incongruous little figures, one all in black and one in vivid chartreuse, so alike and separated only by age and experience, walked upstairs together.

They passed the room at the front of the house where Pearl Angove lay sleeping quietly. Lily stopped outside the door but there was no sound, the cries and sobbing of Pearl's early nights at No 3 Trewavas Terrace less frequent now, the days filled with learning to live the kind of life to which a woman of her age might reasonably aspire.

Lily knew better than to expect Pearl Angove to change her asperity of tongue but there was a moderation in her views, a slackening in her watchfulness and Lily saw a personality, long submerged, beginning to emerge; a character where humour and individuality were rediscovered and perseverance, for so long Pearl's strongest weapon, used to create rather than just to endure.

Pearl had looked around and saw where she might earn some money. She took two cleaning jobs in an area of the town where she went unrecognised and she was looking forward to the summer when she intended to supplement her pension by working in a tearoom on the promenade.

Pearl Angove had discovered in time that life was worth living. She was learning to be happy and resolutely denied the Reverend Wilfred any of her small store of compassion as she watched with detachment his efforts to control his parish without her.

Carol gave her aunt another kiss on the cheek and went quietly up to her bedroom on the top floor, leaving Pearl to her undisturbed sleep.

13

December

Binnie and Enys were to be married before Christmas, Binnie's scruples about marrying in Advent set aside when she realised that she would, in any case, have to marry Enys in a Registry Office.

'If you mind terribly we could try and find someone who'll marry us in church but it might be difficult,' Enys had said and Binnie had thought about it, not answering him quickly, trying to decide if it mattered to her any more and deciding that it didn't. If she had any lingering feeling of disloyalty to her upbringing in the Church she had come to recognise that was all it was. Her faith as she now understood it was incomplete, but such a fundamental part of her life that to suspend all belief was to deny a part of herself as real as her inability to enjoy loud and boisterous parties.

Once Binnie had understood this she told Enys that she was perfectly happy to marry him anywhere, and the sooner the better. They had exchanged looks as she said this and Binnie had added, 'We'd better tell Jory first and then I'll go and see Katha. I do hope she can hang on long enough to be a witness. Are you going to ask James to be the other?'

'I thought so as he seems to have been the catalyst in most of this.'

It was a dry, breezy morning when Binnie went to Rosmorran, the thin high clouds driven fast across a sky of so pale a blue that it looked bleached. The hedges appeared to be dead, black fingers held over their faces to give just a glimpse of fields patchy with mud and roads like unfolded metal. It had been raining for days, heavy squalls rushing in off the sea dragging high tides after them but now the winds seemed to be resting, gathering strength for another assault. It was the time of year when waves crashed and roared over sea walls and railings, tossing ships onto rocks and when the rockets were launched from the Lifeboat station to call the volunteers to duty, they alerted the whole town to danger in its midst.

An ash tree had fallen across the drive to Rosmorran so Binnie had left her car on the grass verge and walked up to the house, passing one of Casey's men on a tractor on his way to divide and drag the broken tree out of the road. As Binnie neared the house she wondered why the smell from the stables always seemed so strong after rain and walked along the line of loose boxes to look at Navaho. His box was empty and she remembered that he was probably out hunting and she suddenly thought of Richard but with no regret, all the pain of his faithlessness gone, transformed into a tolerable memory by her love for Enys.

Binnie floundered through the mud of the yard to the back door of the house, leaving her heavy shoes in the porch before opening the door and calling out to Katha. Katha was uncomfortable and impatient with her discomfort. She refused to sit down and walked around the kitchen, mug in hand, full of complaints and more than usually fierce.

'Sit down just for a bit Katha.' Binnie caught hold of her arm and led her to the farmhouse chair by the side of the Rayburn. 'I want to talk to you and it's very offputting, you wandering about like that. Sit here, it's really quite comfortable and I'll get you the footstool.' Binnie disappeared into the passage to the front of the house and came back with a three legged milking stool which she put under Katha's feet. 'That better?'

'It's better, but nowhere's comfortable. I feel totally foul: varicose veins, piles. I ask you, piles of all ghastly things *and* having to pee every two minutes. Oh why did I ever start this?'

'It's a bit late for that and it's not for much longer now anyway. That's what I came to talk to you about; Enys and I are getting married in three weeks, can you hold out that long do you think because I do need you to be a witness?'

'Well, at least you're not expecting me to be a bridesmaid, I'd have looked good in sprigged muslin like this.'

'You look blooming Katha, not half as bad as you pretend. It's only going to be you and Casey, and James and Jory. James is giving us a luncheon afterwards at Owles Court and I do so want you to be there.'

'Wild horses – and certainly not a baby – wouldn't keep me away, I want to be quite sure you go through with it. But Binnie, don't be cross, but you *do* realise don't you that a lot of people are going to think that it's just a *tiny* bit soon after – you know?'

Binnie looked at Katha sitting uncomfortably in the big chair. 'If I were a man you wouldn't say that. It wouldn't even occur to you, probably think me quite restrained to have waited a year.'

'You *are* cross!'

'Yes, I am. Oh, not with you Katha, but I suppose the next thing will be "what will people say?" I really don't mind what anyone says and I'm surprised at you, you've never given a damn for anyone else's opinion.'

'Not quite true,' Katha said, surprisingly unruffled, 'perhaps, though, I shall when this emerges.' She put her hand on her stomach, 'Or had you forgotten?'

'Of course I hadn't forgotten but why should you worry about that anymore? I thought that you'd managed to sort things out with Casey.'

'Oh that's all right, but what I never told you was that my little fling, my absolutely last little fling it was going to be, was with a very young man who wasn't exactly what you would call "white".'

'Oh God, Katha, you *are* a fool.' They looked at each other and suddenly began to laugh the laughter of transmuted tears.

Katha wiped her eyes. 'For the first time ever I do feel rather ashamed you know. Casey's been an absolute brick, never asked any questions and I know without him saying anything that he'll accept the baby even if it comes out khaki.' She tried to find a more comfortable position, pulling at the cushion covered in cat's hairs which was propping up her back. 'He's so kind Binnie and I've been really vile to him sometimes but can't you understand, I need him to fight me, not be so frightfully *good* all the time.'

'I think that's what Aunt Vee would have called "the cross you have to bear" and I think you should be jolly thankful that's all it is. You know Casey adores you Katha, he's never looked at anyone else and he loves you just as you are. Has he *ever* tried to stop you doing what you want?' Katha shook her head. 'Well then, just accept how lucky you are. But perhaps the little flings should stop?'

'Absolutely. Never, never again. I'm going to be an ideal wife in future,' Katha said but she knew that Binnie didn't understand her need for excitement or the difficulty she would have in keeping her word.

'Now that *might* worry Casey. Worry us all if you change too much.' Binnie was feeling sleepy in the heat of the kitchen and the sky outside was darkening, promising another onslaught of rain. 'I'd better go, I left my car on the road because of the tree down in the drive and there seems to be such a lot to do in three weeks because I'd like Court Farm to be reasonably habitable by the time I move in.'

As Binnie reached the back door she turned towards Katha with her hand on the latch. 'Katha, just now you said that perhaps it was a tiny bit early for Enys and me to get married. Well, actually, it's just about two months too late.' She gave Katha a look that would have surprised those who thought they knew Binnie Seaton and slipped through the door before a stunned Katha could say a word.

Binnie could hear the whine of the chain saw as she walked towards the road and she stopped to talk to Casey as the pearly grey trunk was parted and bound with chains to be pulled clear of the drive.

'How d'you think Katha is?'

'Bad tempered but pretty well I should say. Just keep her on her feet for another three weeks Casey, and once the wedding's over she can have the baby anytime.'

Casey looked seriously at Binnie. 'I'm more pleased for you and Enys than I can say. Richard was never good enough for you Binnie and from what I've seen of Enys, he seems a stayer, a really decent kind of a fella.'

'He is, Casey.' Binnie was amused, as if Casey were judging Enys on his potential as a hunter. 'He is a decent kind of a fella.' She had to stretch up to kiss Casey's cheek. It was rough and he ran his hand over it, pulling a face.

'I was up most of the night with Kilipi. Don't like mares foaling at this time of the year but she got out and by the time we got her back it was too late.' He put his hands in the pockets of his stained waxed jacket. 'Sounds like the story of my life, wouldn't you say?'

Casey looked at Binnie and Binnie said softly, 'You're a really decent kind of a fella too, Casey. One of the most decent and Katha knows it. She's really going to try she says and with a new baby to look after I shouldn't think she'll have time for any distractions.'

They both knew that the words that were left unsaid would never be spoken by either of them and Casey's, 'Goodbye, dear Binnie,' was an acknowledgement of their agreement. As Binnie walked to her car she could see him standing taller than anyone, and as she passed the knot of black-budded branches being swept along behind the tractor he waved and smiled and she felt absolved, able at last to acknowledge to herself that her infatuation for Casey May had been just that, a fantasy she no longer needed now that her life had been completed by Enys' return.

On the morning of the wedding Katha woke with an absolute certainty that her baby was going to be born that day. Early the previous morning Casey had found her in the stables, wearing an old coat of his father's and Casey's own wellington boots. 'What in God's name are you doing Katha? You should ask Cherry or one of the girls if you need something. Come on in now and sit down.' Katha had let him take her into the house but had insisted on cooking breakfast for all of them.

She had worked all day, tidying drawers and sorting through clothes and magazines, Cherry threatening to call Casey if Katha persisted in trying to clean out the cupboard under the stairs. 'That baby'll be here drec'ly, be a race between that and Mrs Seaton's wedding I reckon.'

Katha woke early the next morning and looked at the

clock beside the bed. Casey was still asleep, only his red hair showing above the duvet pulled up over his shoulders. Five hours to the wedding and Katha recognised the ache in her back. She tried to lie quietly so that Casey wouldn't be disturbed, very conscious that they had just passed their last night of uninterrupted sleep for the foreseeable future. She rolled out of bed and went downstairs to make a cup of tea, letting the bad tempered cat out into a damp, misty morning. The sky was pale in the east and pearls of moisture dripped from the slate roof of the old dairy, rustling and stamping coming from the loose boxes across the yard.

It was still cold and Katha went back into the house wondering if Binnie were awake, envying her the certainty with which she was preparing to marry Enys. She thought about Richard and how she had always resisted his advances, loyalty to Binnie overcoming her usual intemperance and she wondered if Binnie had been right to stay with him when she had always been in love with someone else.

Casey came into the kitchen. 'Are you all right Katha?'

Katha looked at him for a long time and then she said, 'A year ago I'd have said that I knew everything about Binnie but I didn't Casey, I really didn't. And she didn't know about me either. Isn't that strange? A year, just over, since Richard died and everything's changed.'

Casey put his arms around Katha. 'Things are changing for us that's true, but we'll be all right Katha, we always will be, whatever happens.' He felt her tense in his arms. 'Are you sure you're OK?'

'Only five hours to the wedding and I'm absolutely going to be there. Don't say a word to anyone Casey, promise, just have the car ready for a swift getaway.'

'Anything we should do?'

Katha took a deep breath and shook her head and went slowly upstairs to shower.

* * *

Binnie was wearing deep, dusky yellow in her favourite style, a long skirt and a long, loose jacket. Her pale hair was uncovered and she had a posy of mimosa which she had handed to Katha, thinking as she did so that Katha looked very strained and hoping that it wasn't all too much for her. Afterwards they drove back to Owles Court, James taking Binnie and Enys in his old navy blue Bentley and Jory riding with the Mays.

It was less than two weeks before Christmas and the house was decorated as it had been in the days when the Seaton family still lived there. There was a fire in the hall and a tree hung with the decorations which Enys remembered seeing as a child. They had been old then and they looked fragile and beautiful, glass globes from which most of the glitter had worn away and there was a fairy with white, spun glass hair and little, sparkling silver shoes. Great candelabra stood waiting to be lit, their light softening the holly and ivy threaded with old, tarnished tinsel.

'Honestly Katha, why didn't you tell me, you are so silly.'

'I told you I'd be here and I've managed the important bit; you're well and truly married and I do hope you'll be ecstatically happy with your Enys.'

Lunch was over and they were sitting on a small oak settle in the hall and although the fire was bright, the afternoon was beginning to darken into an early evening. There were no lights on except tiny white candles on the Christmas tree and the shadows of the two women converged and separated as they flickered over the walls. Katha gave a gasp and reached for Binnie's hand, holding it tightly for a little while.

'I don't think we're the kind for ecstasy really, but – oh Katha, hang on, is it too awful?'

Katha made a face, 'Not too bad.'

Binnie looked up at the sound of laughter: Enys and Jory were walking together down the stairs. Just for a moment as they reached the window on the half landing they were silhouetted against the last of the setting sun and Binnie caught her breath. Two faces so similar one could have been superimposed on the other and both fused into one. They moved on down the stairs and as Binnie turned back to Katha, their eyes met. 'Did you guess?'

'Oh, ages ago but I didn't *understand* for a long time.'

'It was when you were in Canada,' Binnie said, 'I told you that I was pregnant and because I married Richard you came to the same conclusion as everyone else and I let you go on thinking that he was Jory's father. It just seemed easier for everyone really.'

'I know that now but I can't get over you never saying a word. All the letters we wrote to each other and you managed to keep it a secret.'

'Yes I did,' gently, 'that was about the only thing I didn't tell you though.' Binnie was watching Katha trying to feel what she might be feeling, ready to offer support in her discomfiture. 'Do you remember years ago, when we were about eleven or twelve and we promised to tell each other everything? What you called our "utter, utter secrets"?' Katha nodded. 'Well, I could say that I had my fingers crossed but it wouldn't be true but I don't believe I ever intended to tell anyone everything and although you've given a good impression of someone with total verbal incontinence over the years, you're really just as selective as anyone else with any commonsense.'

Katha was holding tightly to Binnie's hand again and she said between her teeth, 'Does Jory know? He must do, surely?'

'He seemed to understand as soon as he met Enys, and Jory being Jory, he never made a fuss or seemed to feel badly about it.'

'And James?'

'James has always known. I'll tell you all about it one day, just now you've got better things to do. I really think it's time you were on your way, Katha.'

'Binnie, I wish you could come with me, I don't think I've ever been so frightened in my entire life. What if the baby is . . . isn't? I can't even say it.'

Patrick Noel May was born at one minute to midnight, the longest baby ever to be delivered at the hospital, the nurses teasing Katha about his thatch of red hair.

Binnie had phoned from the airport, where she and Enys were waiting to catch a flight to Italy for their honeymoon. She pushed through crowds of jostling skiers to get to Enys, delight shining in her face. 'It was still our wedding day and it *is* Casey's baby. Oh lucky Katha, she's given him his son.'

Enys was going to ask Binnie what she meant but he looked at the joy in her face and kissed her instead. Some things, he thought, would always be better left unsaid.

∫

Postscript

Among the Christmas cards which the Reverend Wilfred Angove picked up from the worn coconut mat inside the front door of the Minister's House, was one which bore no signature. In place of a message of seasonal greeting he read:

> *Dear Rev. Angove,*
> *Certain facts have come into my possession regarding your treatment of your wife. I am sure you wouldn't want these to become public knowledge so I suggest . . .*

The Reverend Wilfred threw the brightly coloured picture onto the fire, watching as the flame turned green and the blackened paper curled and crumbled into ashes, but he knew it was only the transitory destruction of fear. Unease would become a daily feature of his life, for he knew there would be more demands, threats which he would be unable to dispose of so casually.

While everyone else in Trewavas Terrace gathered together to celebrate Christmas in a spirit of thankfulness and optimism, the Reverend Wilfred Angove prepared to spend his time alone, apprehension his constant companion.